Readers love *Us Three*
by MIA KERICK

"I just fell in love with this story and with these three guys… This is a must read, guys, especially if you're looking for a story about finding true love in the oddest of places…"
—MM Good Book Reviews

"Wow, what a story… This book is full of feelings and emotions, it had me running the gamut on all of them."
—Hearts on Fire

"I was sucked in from the first word on the first page, shocking as it may be to watch/read, and this book still hasn't let me go. I couldn't stop reading…"
—My Fiction Nook

"…this is the kind of story that lingers with you. As a reader, you get hooked on their story and want to see what is next for the boys."
—Sensual Reads

"Really, you should read this book… It is a highly entertaining story, with some great characters, and a truly lovely romance between the three of them."
—Love Bytes

"In *Us Three*, Mia Kerick has written a powerful, emotionally gripping character driven tale… I think the book should be required reading in ALL high schools, and would DEFINITELY recommend it to everyone."
—Mrs. Condit & Friends Read Books

By MIA KERICK

Beggars and Choosers • Unfinished Business
Grand Adventures (Dreamspinner Anthology)
Out of Hiding
A Package Deal
Random Acts

ONE VOICE
Us Three (Published with Harmony Ink Press)
Here Without You

Published By DREAMSPINNER PRESS
http://www.dreamspinnerpress.com

HERE WITHOUT YOU

Mia Kerick

Dreamspinner Press

Published by
DREAMSPINNER PRESS

5032 Capital Circle SW, Suite 2, PMB# 279, Tallahassee, FL 32305-7886 USA
http://www.dreamspinnerpress.com/

This is a work of fiction. Names, characters, places, and incidents either are the product of author imagination or are used fictitiously, and any resemblance to actual persons, living or dead, business establishments, events, or locales is entirely coincidental.

Here Without You
© 2015 Mia Kerick.

Cover Art
© 2015 DWS Photography.
cerberuspic@gmail.com
Cover Design
© 2015 Paul Richmond
http://www.paulrichmondstudio.com
Cover content is for illustrative purposes only and any person depicted on the cover is a model.

ISBN: 978-1-63216-558-9
Digital ISBN: 978-1-63216-559-6
Library of Congress Control Number: 2014920193
First Edition February 2015

Printed in the United States of America
∞
This paper meets the requirements of
ANSI/NISO Z39.48-1992 (Permanence of Paper).

To my awesome assistant Super Beckey White—Where would I be without you? I'll tell you where I'd be—Lost!!

1

NATE'S DIARY

August 22

US THREE'S all divided up now. Casey and Zander are off to college orientation—where they oughtta be—so that ain't no problem. And just sayin', them two wanted me to go with 'em. They said we could get us an apartment, instead of them livin' in the school dorms. They said I could get myself some trainin' at the culinary arts school right near Boston City College, where them two are goin'. Said it'd be so fuckin' great and we could study together every single night and build our future together.

And I wanted to go with 'em so fuckin' bad I could taste it.

But I couldn't….

Couldn't leave my little sister.

Cindy needed me to run interference 'tween her and Uncle Rich since Mom's still in the slammer. Loudmouthed fourteen-year-old girls and angry boozers needed some kind of a buffer zone in the middle of 'em.

So anyhow, I didn't fess up to that shit like straight out in the open or nothin'. Kept on tellin' Casey and Zander I was super into my job pumpin' fuel at the gas station and I was hopin' like hell to get promoted up to cashier at the minimart that was attached.

Woo-fuckin'-hoo. Mini-friggin'-mart cashier—my dream job! But sometimes you gotta say what you gotta say.

Casey and Zander never bought my bullcrap story. Every time I told them I was livin' for the day I could spend 24/7 ringin' in people's beer and toilet paper and shit, they always looked at each other and raised up their eyebrows, like "Yeah, right—tell me

another one, dude." They knew the score—they knew I was stickin'
close by Cindy to protect her.

But finally them two had no choice about leavin' without me, I
guess. Wouldn't change my mind—insisted I was gonna stay home.
So off they went to Boston City College—gonna be each other's
roommates in this classy-ass dormitory place. My Casey's so
fuckin' smart—gonna be a doctor someday, but right now he's a
biology major. And during senior year in high school, Zander got all
sappy about helpin' kids fit in, so he's studyin' to be a guidance
counselor, which I think is cool cuz guidance counselors have the
power to save kids' asses in high school.

Zander'll be a kick-ass guidance counselor.

Casey'll be a top-notch doc.

I'll be a dumbass gas station attendant. A fuel pumper.

And just sayin', I know them two love me. I know I love
them two.

I just couldn't go with 'em.

Maybe I'll take Cindy out to Friendly's for a burger before I
head over to the gas station. Or maybe I'll just hang here in my
room and try to stop missin' them two so fuckin' bad.

ZANDER ZANE'S One Voice Blog Spot—by invite only

Your host, Zander Z

[For the official record, nobody's been admitted to this blog
quite yet, but I *am* thinking about inviting my older bro, Dan, to be
my blog guinea pig. He's so cool, and it'd be a way for us to keep in
touch. Plus he could write shit in the comments section so it
wouldn't be blank, which fucks with my mind.]

MONDAY AUGUST 22

There are three of us in this thing. Yeah, three… no questions
asked.

It just plain wouldn't work without me, Casey, *and* Nate.

And maybe all three of us are dudes... and maybe we're all three in love.

Alert: Stop reading here if you can't open your mind to those facts.

Or better yet, read on.

I challenge you *not* to change your mind when you see how it is with the three of us.

Casey and I are making tracks to the bookstore when he gets out of the shower. Gotta buy books so we can study our butts off, right? Hate for Casey to study his butt off, it's so freaking cute. LOL.

Gotta try to get my mind, and Casey's mind too, off Nate and what he's doing by himself back in our hometown in the sticks of New Hampshire.

Miss the fuck outta him.

Just saying.

CASEY'S REAL LIFE

BY THE middle of senior year at Benjamin Franklin High School, just about everybody at school had figured out our not-so-secret love alliance. In addition, our parents had developed a fairly clear picture of what we were to each other. My parents were basically fine with it, which seemed unlikely, but considering the alternative, their son being in love with two guys was the best option available. They had watched as Nate and Zander literally lifted me out of a deep pit of depression in the middle of my junior year after I'd been bullied, both mentally and physically, beyond the limits of my endurance by the popular girls. Or as I called my tormenters, "the Queen Bees." I'm reasonably certain that Mom and Dad had experienced the normal reservations in regards to their son's threesome love relationship, but instead of making waves, I believe they chose to consider Zander and Nate as bonus sons. As for Zander's mother, she didn't much care what Zander was up to as long as he steered clear of trouble and got decent grades, so she didn't factor in as a big issue for us. Nate's uncle was the only "guardian" of one of us—and

I used that term very loosely when it came to him—who didn't have a clue about the charmingly romantic "throuple"—a combination of three and couple—in which we were involved. But that was a story in itself. Suffice it to say, what Uncle Rich didn't know wouldn't hurt Nate.

The three of us had basically been inseparable for the past year and a half. Every day since the winter of junior year in high school, we sat together in classes and at lunch and drove to school together and then back home as well, when Zander and I didn't have after-school activities. Nate didn't participate in extracurriculars, except for the gay-straight alliance at our school, called One Voice, which he and Zander founded in an effort to support me and other LGBTQ kids at school during junior year. If we didn't have sports or clubs, he usually just dropped us off at home and went straight to work at the Humane Society, where he helped out with the dogs.

The summer before our senior year was like an amazing dream—a time in my life I'll certainly never forget. The three of us were completely infatuated with each other, and we had sufficient time to spend together. Zander and I had part-time jobs at the mall—Zander at the movie theater and me at Abercrombie & Fitch—and we managed to work our hours around Nate's schedule. That was the summer when he started working at the gas station *and* at the Humane Society so he could buy better quality food and clothing for his little sister, Cindy. But we managed to see each other almost every day. And every single day of that summer we all fell a little bit more in love.

Senior year. I was happy at school for the first time ever. School was fun, and I actually *wanted* to go. I loved getting up every day, climbing into Nate's truck, kissing my boyfriends good morning, and then heading for the very place I used to refer to as "hell on earth." And no, we never officially "came out" as being gay *or* as being three boyfriends, because *I* didn't want to, and Nate and Zander respected my wishes. I'd been through a lot during my junior year. I'd been humiliated, not to mention assaulted, for being gay, as well as for being nerdy and different. Residual fear remained in my head and heart. I wasn't willing to expose myself to that kind of scrutiny.

At least not until the senior prom. The three of us went stag. Well, we went "alone-together," as Nate said. Nate and Zander told me they would wear color-coordinated tuxedos, with the single condition that I'd let them dance with me in public. As in the three of us shaking our groove things together. Our "big secret" was out on June seventh. Strange thing was, nobody, not even the teachers, appeared to be particularly shocked by the revelation that we belonged to a loving threesome, or a throuple.

Although Nate had a presence like a bodyguard, I give much of the credit for my feeling of safety at school to Zander and his obsession with the club he started, with Nate's help. One Voice, our school's gay-straight alliance. The existence of One Voice, and the fact that nearly two-thirds of the student population at BFHS had joined, made our school a kinder and gentler place.

Plus there was the fact that Liz Trainer, the girl who had assaulted me so viciously, had been shipped off to a private boarding school way up the northern part of the state. From what my parents had been told by the school's lawyers, she was still dealing with the legal ramifications of her violent actions.

I felt relatively safe at Boston City College too, but it was just Freshman Orientation Week, so I was still being cautious. I wasn't running around waving a rainbow flag or carrying a sign that read, "Polyamory: Love Multiplied," but I *was* comfortable enough to hold Zander's hand as we walked across the quad and to admit he was my boyfriend when asked directly. But it just didn't feel right without Nate. I missed his strong, silent presence. I missed the way—with his hesitant and inarticulate mumblings—he expressed his love so very eloquently to Zander and me.

I was still trying to hide who I was in terms of my sexuality to some extent, but I would stop hiding if it meant I could walk through the quad with one hand in Zander's and the other in Nate's.

I'd take the risk. For Zander and Nate, I would.

ZANDER ZANE'S One Voice Blog Spot—by invite only—not yet for public consumption.

Your host, Zander Z

Zander here.

My main goal in starting up a gay-straight alliance at Boston City College is to make our school community a safer place for everybody—no matter what your sexual orientation or gender identity. To make it so Casey and me can walk through the cafeteria arm in arm and nobody bats an eyelash. And to make Anna and Claire, two girls I met in the almost endless line signing up for Ethics in Education class, able to feel welcome to go to the Freshman Fall Ball as a couple. To stop name calling on the sports fields, and to cut out the use of terms like "faggot" and "bean flicker" and "fudge packer" in regular life, by showing the whole school community how much they sting.

That's a lot to spit out, but it's exactly how I see it.

At BCC I want to take things one step further than I did at Benjamin Franklin High. See, my biggest goal is to encourage a "live and let live" attitude toward *any* type of love relationship that is legal. Can't forget to mention the legal part—it's big-time important. I'm not promoting relationships between adults and minors or any shit like that. What I mean is, if there are three or four (or more) people who want to be together in a romantic relationship, who the fuck cares?

If it works for you and it works for your partner(s), then be my guest.

This directly applies to our "throuple," or so Casey calls it. FYI, as defined by Urbandictionary.com, a throuple is "a threelationship." That is a cute play on words, but it's actually a real fitting expression. A throuple is a relationship with three players— three loving, caring, committed, sexually active participants. And when I say sexually active, I mean only with each other, which is kinda important. I want "us three," as Nate calls our cozy group, to have all the rights and recognitions of other people's love relationships. I wanna be able to sit between them at a Daughtry concert, one hand gripping Nate's big palm and my other hand rubbing on Casey's knee, as we listen to "Waiting for Superman." I wanna be able to take my guys out to the Village Pancake House for breakfast after a night of holding them in my arms, cut off bites of my cinnamon-maple-apple pancakes, and feed them, one by one, with my own fork—and not have it be a big fucking deal.

I held the first One Voice meeting in a physics classroom in the Ledyard Building this morning, as classes haven't started yet. Yeah, One Voice officially opened its rainbow-colored doors on August twenty-third. Yesterday, Casey and I pretty much plastered the campus with flyers advertising the first meeting, and still all I got was nine people—just freshmen and a few upperclassmen who were at school early to help with orientation and registration—and that number included Casey and me. But you gotta start somewhere, and this is where One Voice starts.

2
NATE'S DIARY

August 23 (they only been gone about half a week now)

SO MAYBE this is a bit fucked up, but I'm gonna put it down on paper in black and white, and maybe when I read it back to myself, it'll seem more normal.

Here's the thing. Like Casey says, us three is a throuple. Three dudes in love. Whatever. Cuz I sure as shit love them guys, and nothin's gonna change that. So, yeah. There's two dudes in place A and one dude, alone, in place B. I just figured them two would be gettin' busy in bed in their fancy dorm room whenever they had a chance—cuz that's what guys do, right?

Well, apparently not so much. Last night they Skyped me. There them two were, sittin' all cozy on Casey's rainbow-colored bedspread. The floppy stuffed unicorn that me and Zander gave him for Christmas junior year was propped up behind 'em, starin' at the computer, like it was lookin' right at yours truly. I felt real alone and a little like a loser (fucked-up fact is they only been gone a couple days), but I leaned back on my bed and acted like I didn't give a shit.

Casey said, in this adorable proper voice, "Nate, there's a topic Zander and I feel it's imperative we discuss. It's a matter of great importance." He already sounds like a doctor, and he's only a freshman in college.

Zander was just starin' into the computer at me, sorta studyin' my I-don't-give-a-shit-about-nothin' expression.

"What's such a big friggin' deal, babe? Lay it on me." That was pretty cool soundin', I thought.

"Well, Zander and I want to have a discussion about…. Nate, we want to discuss physical intimacy. In that…."

Even on Skype I could see that two spots on Casey's cheeks had turned bright pink. Looked like he was having trouble spittin' this out. And he was the talker in our throuple.

"Zander and I are here together, without you, and we've talked about this—"

"I expect you two've been goin' to town on each other every night since you got to college and are prob'ly itchin' to strip each other down right now." Both of my guys' eyes popped open wide when I said that.

"Actually, Nate." Zander spoke up cuz it seemed that Casey was suddenly at a loss for words. "We haven't, and we're not gonna."

"Huh?" That just kinda flew outta my mouth. "Come again, guy?"

Casey found his voice. "We aren't going to sleep together unless you're with us. We discussed it, and neither of us think it would feel right." He glanced at Zander, and them two nodded at each other. "We aren't going to *do anything in bed* together until you're here for a visit."

I shook my head, but it didn't help to make sense of what Casey was sayin'.

So Zander took a turn at it. "We are a *threesome*—"

"*A throuple*," Casey corrected him in his bossiest voice. "It's called a throuple."

"Okay, we are a throuple, and we're nothing unless we're all together."

"Ya get horny, right? So why not just hop in one of them two beds together and do what comes natural, huh?" I figured that was a fair question, and in a way it was me sayin' "go for it, you guys." Like I was givin' 'em permission—not that they needed it.

Casey completely ignored my super generous offer. "We're going to sleep in our own beds and wait to be… *close to each other*… until you're here with us."

"So dude," Zander said with a chuckle. "Get your hot ass down to Boston as soon as fucking possible, ya hear me? I wanna get me some."

I wasn't sure whether to laugh cuz I was damned psyched about this little arrangement or to argue with them cuz it was so stupid. "You guys are friggin' crazy."

"Frigging crazy about you, DeMarco," Zander said.

"We really miss you and would love for you to come down here for the weekend. As in, Friday afternoon. Can you *please* come Friday afternoon, Nate? We miss you. I'm not used to being without you and…." Skype sure gave a damned clear picture. I could tell that Casey's eyes had got all filled up with tears. I felt like some kinda criminal.

"Okay, okay. I'll see if I can figure out somewhere for Cindy to go this weekend. Don't wanna leave her here alone with my uncle, right?"

"No. Of course not." Casey sucked in a deep breath, like he was tryin' to calm himself down. I had this massive urge to climb right into the computer and take hold of the little dude. I knew how to calm him down real good.

But that's how it got decided that there'd be no funny business unless us three were all together. After we logged off Skype, I felt a little bit less alone and breathed easier too.

Casey and Zander were gonna wait for me.

CASEY'S REAL LIFE

SOMETIMES I get so caught up in my thoughts.

I sat in the far corner of the Donnegan Student Center, sipping a cup of hot chocolate from a paper cup, waiting for Zander to arrive. I always chose this distant corner. For some reason, corners seemed safer to me.

The amount of anxiety I experienced when I left my house had steadily decreased, month by month, ever since I forced myself to return to school after the... after the *incident* that occurred in junior year. The incident with Liz Trainer.

When she beat me to a bloody pulp. Kicked my crotch so viciously it nearly burst.

Back then Nate and Zander had been kind of like superheroes to me. They'd made arrangements with the vice principal and guidance counselor to accompany me around the building until I felt comfortable roaming the halls by myself. In fact, I never had to be alone *anywhere*. Not only did they escort me to classes, they also sat on either side of me at lunch, drove me to and from school, and spent the weekends almost entirely in my living room. In addition, Zander initiated One Voice, our high school's gay-straight alliance, which had over two hundred members by the end of our junior year. And it was a fairly small school. Nate and I participated in the club, and seeing that amount of participation helped restore my confidence in humanity in general and in Benjamin Franklin High School students in particular. But any small reminder—a certain scent, the sound of girls laughing loudly, even the sight of specific types of girls' shoes—could induce a full-blown panic attack.

And to this day, I still suffered with anxiety attacks. In fact, I had one today, right before American Lit. It was because I smelled a certain familiar perfume—brought me right back.

"Hey, dude."

Even though I was expecting him, Zander's voice startled me. I must have jumped half a mile.

"Casey. You okay?"

He and Nate knew me so well. "It was a bit of a tough day, Zander. Everything is new here. It's hard for me to get used to all the changes... and feel safe."

Zander dropped down on the arm of my chair, letting his backpack fall to the floor with a loud thump. "Tell me."

When it came to my emotions, Zander never allowed anything to slide by. If he so much as sensed even slight distress, I was destined for a long and thorough discussion/interrogation.

I swallowed hard. Even though I was totally comfortable with Zander knowing about my hang-ups, it was still difficult to bring myself to talk about them. "Had one of those panic things."

"An anxiety attack?"

Looking up into his concerned amber eyes, I nodded.

"You didn't call me."

"You were in that meeting for education majors, and besides…." I allowed my voice to fade away.

Zander stood up. "I know what you were gonna say. Usually when you have panic attacks, *Nate* talks you off the ledge."

He was right. Talking me off the ledge had become Nate's specialty. I thought about big, burly Nate—a truly gentle giant—and I nodded. Then I sniffed hard in an effort to avoid tears.

"I can help you with that too, you know. When Nate isn't here. But… uh… you wanna call him or something?"

I shook my head emphatically. "No. I'm okay now. And besides, Nate's at work." My voice trembled.

Zander reached out his hand to me, and I took it and then stood up. "Let's head back to the dorm, and you can fill me in on what made you freak out."

I nodded again, and the words just slipped out. "I miss him." I closed my eyes in a further tear-preventative measure. Then I felt Zander's arm wrap around my shoulder and pull me against him. "Hopefully he can come this weekend." I crossed my fingers and made a wish.

All we could do was hope.

3
NATE'S DIARY

August 24

TONIGHT, BEIN' home on the range totally sucked. Just my luck. Both my shit-for-brains uncle and my pain-in-the-ass little sister were in rare form. Right up each other's asses since the second Uncle Rich got home from work. I'm surprised Cindy didn't get her front teeth knocked out, but somehow she always manages to escape gettin' her ass kicked. Mostly it was me who got an ass kickin' in the end. It's like she pisses him off on purpose, knowin' that somebody's gonna have to calm him down, and also knowin' I'm not gonna let it be her.

The night went somethin' like this.

I got home from the gas station at say, maybe four, and Cindy was already there when I got home. She was in one fuck of a suckish mood. She started in on me about how she was the only kid in her group who didn't never have sleepovers. This weekend they were all plannin' an end-of-summer slumber party, I guess. One of her bitchy friends had announced to everybody that nobody was ever invited over here, "Cuz Cindy's house is a shit hole." So when I walked in, Cindy was in some kind of a vacuumin' frenzy, only stoppin' to primp pillows, tryin' to de-shit-hole-ize our house. Like she had a chance in hell at doin' that, since this place is way too far gone.

I said, "So even if we didn't live in a shit hole, you know as well as I do that you ain't gonna invite nobody over here. You won't have 'em here, cuz you know that if he felt the urge, Uncle Rich would tear you a new one for somethin' stupid right in front of your snotty friends."

The kid knew I was right, but Cindy's the type where a good offense is the best defense, or so they say, and she went off on my ass. And then she went off on Uncle Rich's ass as soon as he stepped through the friggin' front door, tellin' him his house is a slum and that he has no class. Bad idea.

I tried to warn her—with my eyes and then with gestures—but Cindy wasn't havin' none of it. When she told Uncle Rich that we were in "dire need" of a brand spankin' new sofa and shiny coffee table, he lost it. And he dove at her. But she knew I was hoverin' close by and I'd save her ass. Which I did by sorta swoopin' Cindy outta Uncle Rich's way.

I'm gonna put it mildly and say the asshole was mighty pissed that he couldn't get his paws on her. I ordered her to go get the fuck into my truck, and I booked it out of there with her as soon as I had a chance. Then me and her made our getaway. Came back at around nine, when we figured Uncle Rich'd have passed out—which he had.

But talkin' sense into that girl wasn't happenin'. Sometimes I think Cindy's mad at the whole world or mad at our mom cuz she's in jail or maybe just mad at me cuz I can't fix things. Whatever it is, she wouldn't listen to no reason. So I headed up to my bedroom, flopped out flat on my bed, and tried to breathe my way through all of my pissed-off-ness. That's when I checked my phone for messages.

"Nate, it's me, Casey. I had… kind of a rough day today. I really miss you, and so does Zander. We want you to come stay for the weekend so much. Please figure something out, Nate. I… I… we need you."

Shit.

But also "yay," you know? Them two still need me. So maybe my mind started scramblin' for possibilities of what I could do with Cindy for the weekend—seein' as Casey, and maybe even Zander, needed me and all.

We have these sorta distant cousins who live outside of Boston. Don't know 'em too good or nothin'. Mom lost contact with 'em ages ago. But Cindy had got along okay with our fourteen-year-old cousin,

Jana, one time at a party after a funeral, back a couple years. Back when Mom was more or less in the picture—not in the pen.

Couldn't believe it when I found the name Terri Monaco in my contacts.

Couldn't believe it more when I made the friggin' call to my mother's—as Casey'd say—"well-adjusted" younger sister. A sister who hadn't talked to my mom in years, thanks to my mom bein' such a friggin' screw-up and her younger sister stickin' to the straight and narrow.

ZANDER ZANE'S One Voice Blog Spot—by invite only

Your host, Zander Z

Let me tell you, when I saw Nate step outta his truck in the parking lot by the student center... well, I got a feeling like I haven't ever had before. And shit—it hadn't even been a full week since I'd seen the dude last. Casey, who was standing beside me, just took off running, and next thing I knew, he was in Nate's arms. And I mean his arms *and* his legs were wrapped around Nate. It was fucking adorable. And after Nate leaned his head down to give Casey a quick kiss, he looked up and over at me. When our eyes met, there was this kind of *zing* feeling that went through me. It started in my fingertips and toes and worked its way into my heart, which sounds like a crock of shit, but there it is. I'm pretty sure neither of us smiled or winked or anything. We just felt each other's presence. And it felt damned good.

Gonna stop here for a second and make a kind of public service announcement. All I can say is that this is a blog, so my plan is that someday I want lots of people to read it to learn about gay love—and about the gay love of *three* dudes. You know, so the world can see that what the three of us have together isn't some nonstop sex fest or some kind of experiment or a joke. It's a real, loving relationship.

We must have stood there like that for a full minute. Nate's big hands roved all around on Casey's back, assuring the little guy that he was really there. And the two of us stared at each other like we'd never seen each other before and we never would again. Finally Casey lowered his legs to the ground and grabbed Nate's hand.

"Come on. Zander needs you too."

Nate smiled when Casey said that.

I met them in the middle and hugged Nate around the waist, saying something like "Good to see ya, man." It barely scratched the surface of what I was feeling, but it was a start.

As we walked together to the dorm, Casey clung to Nate's hand, and I let him because he needed it. My eyes were drawn to them, though. I couldn't stop studying the beauty of the contrast— petite and fragile Casey, light hair and skin, with wide blue eyes like a kid—and Nate, broad-shouldered and muscular, as dark as Casey was light, his long black hair brushed 'til it was smooth and falling around his shoulders. But what kept drawing me in, making me study him, was his eyes. The haunted look that was in them when I first got to know him junior year was back. In a major way.

"You guys musta set up your room real nice by now. Last time I saw it was the day you guys moved in, and shit was everywhere."

"It's *our* room, Nate. Just because you don't live there with us all the time doesn't mean anything. You belong there too."

Casey always said the sweetest shit, and I quickly jumped on that wagon. "Yeah. Casey's right. We pushed the beds together before you got here so we could... you know." I was rambling almost like I was nervous or something.

Nate looked at me and winked. "Can't wait to check out them beds."

I got this tingling feeling—like everywhere. I seriously wanted to run back to the room and beg my guys to run right along beside me, but I played it cool. When we got to the dorm, Casey practically dragged Nate to the second floor where our room is.

"We put pictures of the three of us all over this cork bulletin board that hangs above my desk. And I made all of these little hearts out of pink tissue paper. And we got some huge pushpins, and it looks really good. And over Zander's desk, I hung that peacock feather poster you guys gave me for Christmas junior year—remember it? It makes me feel a little bit better when I'm down and when I'm missing you so badly I think I can't stand it for another minute."

Casey was in full rambling mode. I smiled, and when I looked at Nate, he was grinning too.

STRANGERS ARE going to be reading this someday, and you guys don't know much about our relationship. So in the interest of the blog, I will say that, to this point, although we've been together for about a year and a half, the three of us haven't had sex. Like, yeah, we've fooled around, as in touching. But we haven't gone further than that.

You're probably wondering why the hell not. I mean, it's not like one of us can get preggo or anything. And sure, we're guys, and sure, we get horny. But news flash. We also have this thing called self-control. More than anything else, though, we care about each other, and we *want* to take things slow. *Surprised?* Well don't be. And yeah, you heard me right. Three horny gay guys decided to wait 'til the time is right to have sex. And the time wasn't right in high school.

Nate has now had all the tests to check for sexually transmitted diseases and AIDS and shit, seeing as he is the only one of us who isn't a virgin. **Side note: everybody who has been in a sexual relationship should have these tests.** We've gotten to know and trust each other fully, and we now finally have a chance to be truly alone—no parents or little sisters to interrupt us. The time is coming for us to get closer.

CASEY'S REAL LIFE

I WAS so gloriously, deliriously happy to have Nate with us that I actually couldn't see straight. I also knew I was chattering on and on like somebody had wound me up and let me go, but I just couldn't help myself. And as far as "Casey's legendary relentless babbling" goes, Nate and Zander had long ago told me that my nonstop chattering was one of the things they loved most about me, so I wasn't self-conscious about my little habit. In addition, I believed them because they were both kind of quiet guys, so somebody had to fill up all of the empty air with words.

All I knew was that I needed to get Nate and Zander together on our newly pushed-together almost-like-king-size bed. I needed to feel their skin surrounding me. The warmth. The safety. I needed to revel in the exquisite feeling of *belonging* that only existed when the three of us were together.

I noticed a subtle change come over Nate when we brought him into the dorm, and it became more pronounced as we passed some guys we knew on the stairs and then in the hallways when we exchanged greetings. He seemed to sort of shrink into himself, and it didn't take a rocket scientist to sense his insecurity. I knew Nate felt like he was somehow less than those of us who were studying for our degrees at college.

So I set my mind to the task of letting him know how worthy, indispensable, and utterly essential he was to Zander's and my happiness.

Thankfully by the time we got to our room, Zander had already taken his key out, so I didn't have to scramble around for mine. He unlocked the door. I couldn't have helped much, as my hands were literally trembling—with anticipation, concern, desire, emotional need. So many emotions were swirling around inside my head it was affecting my coordination.

Nate hesitated for a few seconds before he stepped through the open door. Once he got inside, he looked all around and then said softly, "Your room kicks ass, you guys." I noticed his eyes settled momentarily on that peacock feather poster they had given me right after I was assaulted in high school, as if it were a safe place to rest them.

Zander, who was standing off to the side, stepped behind Nate and closed the door. Then he reached up, put his hands on the back of Nate's shoulders, and squeezed, saying, "Make no mistake about it, dude. This is *our* room. Yours, mine, and Casey's. You just can't be in it all the time."

I looked up at Nate to gauge his reaction, but his face remained stoic, as if he hadn't heard what Zander said. I knew he needed physical proof that we were still *all his*. He didn't have anybody but us and Cindy, and knowing we belonged to him meant everything to him. I took his hand and led him to the bed, but before I pushed him down, I reached up and started unbuttoning his flannel shirt. His dark eyes were wide as he stared almost stonily across the room, in the direction of Zander's desk. I knew he was trying to adjust to the intense emotions.

Within thirty seconds, Zander had his hands on Nate's belt and then on the button fly of his worn jeans. We had our man stripped to his wrinkly cotton boxers in less than two minutes. Then together we pushed him down on his back on the bed, and I heard a very un-Nate-like whimper come from his lips.

"We got ya, dude," Zander said as we surrounded him, but Nate protested.

"Nah… no, want Casey 'tween us two." I could tell he had trouble croaking out the words.

Who am I to argue?

I pulled off my polo shirt and my khakis, and boom, I flopped down in the middle of Zander and Nate. I took hold of both their faces, one in each hand, and I looked from Nate to Zander and then back. "Oh my God, I love you guys so much and…."

A few tears escaped the corners of my eyes, but I didn't care. The blissful feeling of being completely surrounded by my guys was too much to stay dry-eyed. And looking at their yearning faces, I could tell I wasn't the only one needing more.

"You got too many clothes on, Zane." Nate somehow found the presence of mind to wink at Zander. "Strip down, bud."

For once Zander wasn't coy. He yanked off his jeans first and then threw his T-shirt onto the floor in a heated rush. He was sort of panting already. It had been a while since we'd been intimate, and he was needy. Okay, *I* was needy, and from the look of the pup tent in Nate's boxers, he was needy too.

So I broke the ice and asked with a grin, "What are you guys waiting for?"

That's when their lips descended on me.

Zander went straight to my lips, while Nate took the roundabout route, licking my earlobe with the tip of his tongue, sliding his mouth down to that sensitive spot behind my ear, and then tasting the hollow beneath my chin. Zander's lips worked mine almost roughly. I felt like the victim of a ravenous feeding frenzy, and no, that was not a complaint.

"Kiss me, Nate." Zander's voice was gravelly and rough, and he craned over me to get a taste of Nate's mouth. Nate was happy enough to comply, and I'm pretty sure I allowed my own soft whimper of approval to escape as I watched them kissing just above my chest.

"Too horny, might come already…."

I was surprised to hear that confession from Nate. He was usually the last one of us to achieve orgasm, always making sure we were satisfied before he allowed his own satisfaction.

Tonight was gonna be different, and it seemed Zander agreed. "Well, that's not a problem, Nate. Let's all come quick this time and then chill with it the second time around."

Nate and I nodded eagerly, and I slid my hands into my boyfriends' boxers. In short order, their hands were on my privates, stroking and exploring. I had the best end of the deal.

And for the first time ever—maybe it was because we were sexually needy but more likely because we were desperate for each other's very presence—our three mouths came together at once. There was no rhyme or reason to our kissing. Our tongues were out, and we just rubbed them together with wide-open mouths and made all kinds of sounds, ranging from gasping breaths, to low moans, to phrases like "don't stop," "missed ya," and "feels good."

Nate and Zander bucked their hips up into my hands, and I followed suit into their hands, though I got to push into one tight fist while another hand cupped my balls. I wasn't sure who was doing what to me. It really didn't matter. Soon we were all losing it, releasing into each other's hands. And then all at once we took a mutual, deep "after the climax" breath, which was almost as good as the big event itself.

The only sound in the room was that of the heavy breathing of three satisfied men. And since everybody knew I would speak first, I did. "Oh, my fucking God."

I'd swear I felt the air rush past my face as two heads jerked toward me at once.

"You don't never curse, Casey." Nate offered an astute observation as he gawked at me with an open mouth.

"I guess I don't," I admitted.

Then Zander chimed in. "So what the hell was *that* all about?" I knew he wasn't disappointed in my foul language, because he asked it with a smile.

"It's just so good to be with you guys like this—like I'm lost in a combination of love, need, and relief, you know? I thought the use of the word 'fucking' was called for in this circumstance."

Nate and Zander laughed out loud, and that's when Sexual Round Two started up.

WE ATE dinner at College Pizza. Nate insisted on paying, as he was the one with both a full-time and a part-time job. Nate and I sat on one side of the booth, with Nate on the outside, across from Zander, so he could stretch out his long legs in the aisle

"So where's Cindy this weekend?" I could tell by Zander's devious expression that he was doing something naughty to Nate under the table with his foot.

"She's with my aunt and cousins. Didn't much think she was gonna go for it, right? But finally she said she'd go, after Aunt Terri told her she was takin' Jana to the mall. Cindy was like, 'I'm in.'" He closed his eyes and gasped when he finished explaining, and I figured Zander's foot had reached the sensitive spot, high on Nate's inner thigh.

"Thank God for that. An offer to go to the mall *is* very difficult to say no to." I loved going to the mall too, but with premed studies, I hadn't been to a mall in ages.

Nate and Zander stared at me for a second, because they *hated* the mall.

"I forked out a bunch of cash, and she was all pumped." Nate spoiled his little sister a lot.

"What really matters is that she isn't alone with Rich." Zander spoke, his lips curling with obvious distaste. He hated Nate's Uncle Rich ten times more than he hated the mall.

Nate nodded, chewing a bite of his spicy chicken barbeque pizza. "Can't have none of that. He'd slap her silly if she started in on him."

Zander and I exchanged conspiratorial glances, because we'd discussed this situation a few times over the last couple of days. We were both of the opinion that Cindy often riled up her uncle and let Nate take the fall. We just weren't sure why she did that. But we kept our mouths shut about it and finished up the last of two pizzas. I personally preferred the chicken Alfredo with spinach pizza pie, but Zander and Nate had each chowed down on both flavors like starving men.

"How's shit with your uncle and you, man?"

I had been wondering if Zander was going to ask that.

Shrugging, Nate said, "Fair, I s'pose. Ain't got no black eyes, right?" He chuckled a bit. Zander and I just gawked at him.

"Nate, he can't treat you like his perfect little punching bag. You need to tell us if he lays a finger on you... or Cindy." Zander was mad, I could tell. "And speaking of Cindy, man. She gets him pissed off, and then you have to take the ass-kicking so she doesn't."

Nate shrugged again, and again Zander and I caught eyes.

"What's up with that, huh? You've done everything for her."

Zander was getting worked up, and Nate was quickly retreating into his own head.

"Maybe she thinks I haven't done enough or somethin'. Guess you'd have to ask her."

Sometimes Nate got into this inexpressive mode when we pushed him too hard for details and promises about his uncle and his little sister. So I grabbed his shaggy head and pulled it down to my lips. Before I kissed his scruffy cheek, I whispered, "We only ask because we're crazy about you." He nodded once, and I planted a wet one on him, which landed right under his eye.

"So, my man, we got us some big plans for tonight." Zander had put a lot of effort into making this weekend fun. Lately he'd turned into such an organizer.

"College parties and shit?" Nate tilted his head and wrinkled his nose.

Zander reached across the greasy table and scooped up Nate's big hand. "You think we'd finally get you all to ourselves and then cart you off to some beer bash where we'd have to share you with a hundred drunks?"

"Umm… you'd better think again, boyfriend." I giggled a little as I spoke.

"Plus, Nate, we don't waste our time at parties. I know I did enough of that shit in high school before I hooked up with you two. Don't miss it one bit."

I hadn't ever been exactly *invited* to a party, so I had nothing to add except, "Zander is kind of obsessed with launching One Voice at BCC. Last Friday *and* Saturday night he was staring at his laptop all night making plans and—"

"I *did* launch One Voice. Maybe it's off to a modest start, but it exists now. That's the first step."

"I told you, Nate, we had nine people at the first meeting, including us. But this Sunday… this Sunday there will be *ten*, we hope."

Nate took a large sip of root beer and gave no indication he had a clue what I was suggesting.

"Nate, on Sunday you're coming to the meeting, right?"

He shook his head, and his long dark hair flew from side to side. "Nah, them college kids don't want nothin' to do with the likes of me."

At hearing those words, Zander practically yanked Nate right over the table. "Shit, DeMarco, the group is called *One fucking Voice*. The students in it are trying to *connect* people, not tear them apart."

He abruptly let go of Nate's hand, and I was pretty sure he was frustrated. We'd worked so hard over the past year to prove to Nate he was worth our effort, and it seemed like Nate had forgotten it in the week we'd been gone.

"Let's get outta here." Zander turned and headed for the door.

Nate and I slid out of the booth, and I told him quietly, "Zander will feel better after we eat our make-your-own sundaes. And that's a major clue as to where we are going next." I grabbed his hand, and we caught up to Zander.

4

NATE'S DIARY

August 29

STELLAR WEEKEND. Fuckin' hated like hell for it to be over. Had to pretty much drag myself away from them two. Cuz it's like this—us three friggin' belong together.

Yeah. So I said it. That don't make it real, though.

Thought I stuck my foot in it real deep on Friday night at College Pizza with Zane. Seems I managed to piss him off big time, but thank Christ, we worked it all out and we got to keep on goin' with our stellar weekend.

When I first got there on Friday, see, them two had me in bed before ten minutes was up. Nope, not complainin'. And damn, we stayed there for a long while, cuz it was super monumental being together again—stayed in the bed 'til we were all three starvin', that is. Yeah. Our grumblin' bellies finally got us outta bed. We went for pizza at this college pizza joint. Little pockets of preppy college dudes were sprinkled here and there, gapin' at me like they never before seen a redneck. I got to feelin' like a piece of shit without no reason in life, and I said some stupid shit about One Voice. If you want to piss off Zander Zane, you dis his precious love-everybody-equal rainbow group.

And before that, Zander brought up the whole fucked-up thing goin' on with Uncle Rich and Cindy and how I'm forced to pay for her sins. And I don't know what to make of her actions neither, so I figure it must be my fault somehow. And I guess I didn't give Zane the right answers to his real good questions on the topic.

But thank shit we got back on the right track at the make-your-own-sundae joint that looked like some kinda Hansel and Gretel gingerbread house on the outside. That part was all thanks to Casey, who kept on grabbin' my hand as we were eatin' our ice cream and stickin' it on top of Zander's hand, over and over, so any ice that'd formed 'tween me and Zander got melted away.

Our ice cream sundaes came out lookin' a lot like each of us. Casey's was small and perfect, a strawberry sundae with one scoop of vanilla ice cream that turned pinkish with the strawberry sauce, a tiny puff of whipped cream, and a pretty strawberry right on top. Zander made himself a decent-sized butterscotch sundae, also with vanilla ice cream. But he skipped the whipped cream and went with a pile of crushed-up nuts instead. Then there was my ice cream sundae. It turned out to be an enormous and towerin' pile of a bunch of different kinds of ice cream, hot fudge *and* butterscotch sauce, whipped cream, jimmies, nuts, tiny chocolate candies, a bunch of these spicy little red hearts, a couple of cherries, and two biscotti stuck into the side of the bowl. Casey told me that's what them crispy cookies were called. Like, you name it and it was in that bowl. Big and not too pretty, it was.

Us three sat in that cute old-fashioned-lookin' ice cream parlor and downed those sundaes, not talkin' too much like we did at dinner, but more just eatin' and takin' each other in. Casey was as cute as ever. He insisted on feedin' each of us a big spoonful of his strawberry sundae, and then he stole bites of our ice cream right off our spoons. I rubbed Zander's knee a couple times to let him know that *I* knew wherever and however One Voice met would be a good and kind place where I would belong.

After ice cream, there were movies. And after movies was the best part, when we got back to the dorm. Us three went to the big bathroom in the hallway, and we lined up at this long row of sinks and brushed our teeth while lookin' at each other in this stretched-out mirror. We each took a minute in the can, and then we headed back to the room. I'm supposed to be callin' it "our room," but it feels too weird, so I just call it "the room."

That night in bed we did somethin' a little different from what we usually do. First, I got on my knees and told each of them to lie down on their backs on each side of me. Casey lay right down, but Zander looked at me sideways for a couple seconds before he slowly leaned back. Didn't bother me none. I knew it was a bit harder for him to give up all sexual control to me when I wanted it—much more than it was for Casey—but that inside his heart, he really wanted to. So, soon as they were both lyin' there, holdin' on to each other's hands and lookin' up at me, I took hold of their dicks and just did my thing. Told 'em they had to look up at me the whole time I was doin' it too.

I'm not lyin' when I say I saw the prettiest expressions I ever seen on them two faces. Those guys just lay there and took what I gave 'em—their honest eyes wide open and gazin' up at me. Casey had lots of trouble stayin' still toward the end. He kept on thrustin' his hips up to help me out with what I was doin'. Who could blame him? Still, I told him to settle down, cuz I had it all under control. But he kept those baby blues of his locked right on me. Now Zander didn't have no problem keepin' his ass still on the bed. He let me do as I wanted to him, but he kept on closin' his eyes every time he got to feelin' real good, like he wanted it to be his own private thing. And wanna know what? I kept right on sayin', "Zander, look at me," every time them eyelids of his slipped shut. And the fucked-up thing is, he listened to me. Struggled a bit but opened those amber eyes and gazed up at me. I saw hella trust in both sets of eyes.

Saw trust in those eyes, the love there, the missin' me, and the gladness that I was there with them, pumpin' their dicks without mercy. This next thing is gonna sound like a pile of crap, but what the fuck. Gonna spill it anyhow. Seein' that love, I almost lost it in two different ways. First of all, I almost cried. Held back, but it took everythin' I had to keep my eyes dry. And second, I nearly came. Yup, just touchin' my guys—lovin' them with my hands and eyes—had me ready to shoot.

Speakin' of shootin', I had both of my guys firin' off at the very same second. Timed it right, I did. And they didn't waste no time draggin' me down 'tween the middle of 'em and stickin' their hands inside my shorts. Soon I was goin' off myself.

I hadn't slept with my guys naked many times before, mostly cuz when we slept overnight together back in high school, we were at Casey's house. And sure, we all slept together on the floor of Casey's bedroom plenty of times—Casey called it *a nest* that we made outta all the blankets—but not bare-assed. That night, after we cleaned ourselves up, we slept without no clothes on. We put Casey's soft body 'tween us, and I pulled his back against my chest. As I had long arms, I tugged Zander toward us so he was chest to chest with Casey, and I had my hand on the back of his neck.

It was a fuckin' slice of heaven.

Last thing I remember before we fell sleep was hearin' Casey's sweet voice sayin', "Wish you never had to leave, Nate."

And then Zander. "Then we could be like this every night."

Yeah. Don't I fuckin' wish it?

ZANDER ZANE'S One Voice Blog Spot—by invite only

Your host, Zander Z

Warning. I know this is a blog, and someday it will be read by others, but I'm not going to spare the personal details about my feelings for my partners. These are the very details necessary to make the very first members and creators of One Voice real to you and thus make One Voice, itself, real to you. And so on that note—

IT WAS so fucking hard to let go of Nate on Sunday night. I swear, a part of me wanted to pack up my shit and head home to NH right along with him. But another part of me asked where that would get us. Casey and I need to study so we can get good jobs. Only then will we be able to take Nate and Cindy away from that asshole, Rich, and help get Nate on track for his own future career. The dude wants to be a cook. Ever since the three of us first got to know each other in our junior year of high school by doing a French project together, Nate has been fascinated with cooking. And he's a decent cook—no joke. If you ever read this, Nate, your crepes are the best!

Casey and I have talked about this plan a lot, and we've decided that we'll help to get him enrolled in a nearby cooking school at the earliest opportunity.

So, all three of us went to the One Voice meeting on Sunday. It was the last thing we did together before Nate had to pick up his little sister at his aunt's house and make the trip back to New Hampshire. Before the meeting, Nate got real quiet, and Casey and I had no trouble figuring out exactly why. We knew the dude, and we knew he always fought feelings of low self-esteem, especially in the academic department. Boston City College was an academic environment, and Nate felt out of his element.

Casey and I had thought we'd fixed these insecurities in Nate over the course of last year, our senior year in high school. We'd studied together an embarrassing amount, and as a result, Nate's grades had skyrocketed compared to his freshman and sophomore years. Fact is, dude, if you're reading this, you're supersmart, and the only one who doesn't know it is you. Just saying.

But Nate slipped back into his old insecurities quick enough.

So even before we headed over to Ledyard Hall, Nate was basically silent and sulky, and it was clear that he was suffering from his old insecurities to the umpteenth degree. But I didn't let him off the hook and say "Why don't you skip the meeting and head home now?" *I* wanted him there. *We* needed him to be there. *He* needed to be there with us.

So we dragged him over to the meeting, and as I expected, we only got five returning members, not including us. I guess two of the kids who'd come last week either had other plans or weren't committed to the concept.

"Well," I joked as the three of us entered the classroom. "Our first task is going to have to be a focus on recruitment, huh?"

My five loyal members, along with Casey and Nate, laughed a bit uncomfortably. Then we pushed the tables to the sides of the room and formed our chairs into one circle. Once we were all facing each other, I made an announcement.

"And so, in the interest of openness and out of the love and pride I feel in my relationship, I'd like to officially introduce to you my family. You have already met my partner, Casey. And now I would like to introduce you to *our* partner, Nate."

Yeah. The room was pin-drop quiet for a full minute, and I noticed Nate had turned alarmingly pink. I also noted that Casey reached over to where Nate was sitting in the chair beside him and took his hand.

"I hope that Nate will be able to be here for many, in fact, for *most*, Sunday evening meetings to offer his support and help to the cause—acceptance of everyone's sexual orientation and choice of partners."

Five sets of staring eyes slid from me to Casey to Nate and then fixed on me again. One by one, they nodded. Small nods—but nods nonetheless, except for one dude.

"That's fucked up," he said, and then got up and left. Casey turned bright red, and I worried he might bolt too, but Nate hung on to his hand, which kinda settled him down. As long as I knew Casey, though, he hated to be the subject of controversy, because being noticed in a negative way made him feel like a target. At that moment, I was more glad than ever that Nate was with us.

One girl thankfully muttered, "To each his or her own," as he walked out, and, armed with that hint of approval, I figured it would be best to get our minds on the business at hand.

"I wasn't joking when I said that recruitment would be our first task. And I feel confident that we'll capture the interest of the LGBTQ community here at school if we make ourselves noticeable enough. But I'm not satisfied with that."

I am sure that Casey and Nate knew exactly where I was going with this, but I got more "this guy is warped" looks from the rest of the small group. The four of them were examining me as if I was a science experiment, which might not seem super overwhelming in terms of numbers, but they *were* the majority.

"Everyone here, as well as everyone on campus, deserves to have his or her sexual orientation and gender identity respected. This cannot happen without straight allies." I took a deep breath and then glanced at Casey, who made an effort to smile, and Nate, who winked. I felt empowered by their responses. "Now, we've all known the bullies who make people feel unwelcome and somehow 'less,' based on their perceived sexual orientations. And we've all seen *or been* their victims too. In order to shut down these bullies, who thrive on disenfranchising others to feel empowered, we need the bulk of the community, LGBTQ *and* straight, to participate in our club—to buy into our objectives and to support us when it counts."

When had I started sounding like a politician?

An athletically built girl with buzzed platinum hair raised her hand and then spoke before I could even acknowledge her. "So, I'm Britta, in case you all forgot my name, and I'm a junior. I'm more than glad that you're starting this alliance up here at school. God knows, it's necessary. I tried to start one of these groups in high school, and I got no response from the straight kids. As in, none. They weren't *for* us, and the distance they kept made me feel like they were *against* us. Eventually, the club—that was tiny to begin with—fizzled out completely."

All of the other kids, the female couple from ethics, Anna and Claire, and Jeremy, a junior who looked like he might play football, as well as Casey and Nate nodded.

"I'm down with that, Britta, which is why we need to focus on recruitment. First from the outwardly LGBTQ crowd, but we also need to strike a chord in the hearts and minds of the rest of the student population and with the staff too." I passed out a schedule that I had printed at the library. "This is what I want our first activity as a group to be. To set up a club table in the quad on Saturday, October 1, which is Student Involvement Day, to try to enroll members."

"So we'll be basically 'coming out' to the whole school just by sitting at that table?" Jeremy had a point.

Claire stepped up to respond. "No, Jeremy. It means only that we support a safe school environment for all people. And if none of us is willing to do that, then there will be no change."

The room was stone silent for a moment, and then everybody lifted the papers and studied them.

"All of us are going to have to be at that table pretty much all day. We'll just give each other turns with breaks." I then spelled out the materials we needed to set up the table, designated who would bring snacks and drinks and how we would attend the table all day so it was never empty. Next we looked at the mini-calendar of events I listed at the bottom of the page, outlining days we would hold rallies.

"Our first rally will be on October 11, as it's National Coming Out Day. It's the Saturday before the Columbus Day holiday."

Again Jeremy provided the voice of reason. "So kids are supposed to be lining up at our table in the quad that day to sign up to come out?" I couldn't miss the sarcasm in his voice. "Like, right."

"That won't be our goal. Instead, our goal will still be recruitment. I want to have at least fifteen members by that date and to double our club's enrollment on that very day alone, due to whatever activity we organize to do in the quad."

Claire stood up and looked around at the very small crowd. "We have to be the positive ones, right? If we, the leaders in this movement, can't be positive, then who will be?"

Again the nods, even Jeremy. I went on to point out The National Day of Silence on April 17 and Harvey Milk Day, which would be May 22, one of the last days we would be on campus for finals. "We've gotta fill in the rest of the calendar with our own campaigns to make this thing happen."

Casey and Nate, as predicted, sat quietly beside me as I laid out my plan. I knew Casey believed in the cause. The existence of One Voice was the main reason he came back to school after he was assaulted during junior year. He knew he had support in large numbers from straight and LGBTQ students alike. But Casey's voice was very quiet in the high school One Voice club, and he stayed on the outskirts of the group—involved but reserved. I knew this behavior was caused by the leftover fear that he couldn't get rid of because he'd been targeted by bullies for the majority of his school years. Nate had actually been one of the most involved members in high school, totally down for every event we planned. He'd done a lot of the driving, legwork, and lifting. Once it had become clear to him that his voice was as important as others, he'd even volunteered his thoughts. Not often but often enough.

Now I'm going to take the opportunity to handle this entry as a regular One Voice blog post. So I'll point out a few things that are important. In One Voice, *all* voices—quiet and reserved, lively and determined, questioning and critical—are welcome. Every voice simply represents a population of people whose words or quiet presence needs to be recognized. No matter if you join One Voice to sit, listen, and nod, to carry our table and wave our banner in the quad, or to take charge of an activity, you are vital to making the goals of this club happen.

Everybody who is open minded and welcoming to others, regardless of sexual orientation or gender identity, is welcome here in One Voice. Although we are "One Voice," we are comprised of many varied, individual voices.

5

NATE'S DIARY

August 30

SEEMS LIKE I just can't get my head outta my ass. Nah. What I mean is, I can't figure out how to find that place in my head where it feels like everything's gonna be all right.

It's cuz I *miss* those guys. So I'm mostly sure I ain't losin' my mind or nothin'.

I can feel the missin' 'em in my bones, and it makes my bones ache like I got the flu. It's like I can see my guys in front of my eyes every time I blink. I see 'em doin' their *own* thing, livin' their college lives without me, growin' smarter and better by the second. Even though the smarter part of me knows that ain't what they're doin', cuz they're missin' the hell outta me too. And when I lay in my bed at night, I can smell 'em and taste 'em and hear all of their squeaky sounds when I love them. Just like I was still with 'em. But I'm not.

Casey and Zander. Casey and Zander. My Casey and my Zander.

Them two guys are my life. So how'd I get stuck all alone in this fuckin' small, fuckin' dismal town, two hours north of 'em?

It's like, over and over I have to friggin' remind myself how much Cindy needs me. Gotta tell myself that she needs me here day and night. It seems like I'm feelin' more pissed off about it than I'm feelin' big-brother protective, like I oughtta be. Without me here, let's face facts, Cindy's basically up shit creek, not a paddle in sight. Gotta wonder if she keeps the drama goin' with Uncle Rich just to keep me around. She knows real good that I won't leave her alone here if I think she's in danger.

So I'm gonna drag my ass outta bed, make me and her a decent breakfast, and fake a good-mornin'-how-about-a-glass-of-OJ smile to get her started on the right foot.

Four years. See, it's like this. Cindy's a freshman in high school. I gotta stick it out here, watch out for her ass, for four more years.

Then I can join up with them two in Boston and maybe sort out my own life.

If they still wanna let me join up with 'em at that point.

CASEY'S REAL LIFE

IT WAS turning into a habit. When Zander and I had something monumental to discuss with Nate, we called ahead and set up a "Skype appointment" for when he got home from work. At the agreed-upon time, we'd lean against the wall behind Zander's bed, set up the laptop on his knees, and Skype Nate. We'd hem and haw for a few minutes, make some meaningless small talk for a few more minutes, and then we'd lay the topic, whatever it was, out there.

It felt a bit like two against one. I worried that maybe he would perceive that we were ganging up on him. All we really wanted was to get him here with us permanently and to help him get his life on track.

A couple of nights before, we'd done the whole Skype routine, with the goal of extracting a promise that he'd come to visit us again the next weekend. Last weekend was incredible. It was only natural for us to want an instant replay. There was a football game in the Arthur Johnson Stadium on Saturday and a pancake breakfast at the student center on Sunday morning, both of which we wanted to attend with Nate.

He said he'd try to figure out a plan for where Cindy could go on Friday and Saturday nights. And tonight we would ask him what his plan for Cindy was. Then we were going to fill him in on our other huge, but definitely still tentative, plans.

When Nate turned on Skype and leaned back in his chair, I knew he wasn't doing very well. I knew the signs of depression, having barely survived it myself. He seemed far away, and I didn't mean that he was in New Hampshire and we were in Boston. His dark eyes were glassy and staring off to the left. He wasn't connected with us, and he looked as if he had no inclination to be. He looked skinnier than usual. And very pale.

I knew instinctively that it had hurt him deeply to tear himself away from us on Sunday. His distant behavior was an attempt to cope with his pain. Nate needed us more than I had thought, more than Zander had predicted, more even than Nate knew how to deal with.

"Hey, *sweetheart*." That was a new one for me, but it served its purpose. Not only did Nate shift his eyes from whatever he was staring at in the upper left corner of his bedroom and look toward my face, but Zander too suddenly turned to look at me. "How's my big guy?"

Nate apparently had lost his ability to formulate words.

"Yeah, dude. Whassup in the hometown?" Zander stepped in to help me out.

"Uh… not much." Brief and to the point.

"We've been missing you so much. I can't concentrate on my studying without your hand in my hair." Throughout our senior year, the three of us had studied together in my living room. Most of the time, I would sit on the floor in front of the coffee table, and Nate and Zander would sit next to each other on the couch. Nate spent most of the time rubbing little circles on my scalp.

"Yeah. Well, whatever," he grunted and looked back to whatever was so fascinating in the upper left corner of his bedroom.

Since we were going nowhere fast with our banter, Zander focused our throuple on business. "So, what's the deal with this weekend? Did you find a place for Cindy to stay so you can come here?"

Nate just shook his head.

"Nate, please try harder. We want you to come. I *need* you to come here." I hadn't planned those words—they spontaneously erupted from my lips. "Can't she stay with your aunt again?"

The long dark hair moved from side to side on his wide shoulders as he shook his head again.

"She's got friends. How about if she goes to one of their houses?"

"Zander, I'm friggin' workin' on it." Neither of us had ever heard Nate speak so harshly other than to those who threatened me in high school. For a moment, we were all silent. Awkwardly so. "Shit. Didn't mean to bite your head off, man."

Zander nodded, but his body had stiffened beside me.

"Well, let us know if you find her a place to stay. We really want to see you," I offered. I was ready to move on to the topic of epic proportions, despite the fact that we were having an off moment. "Zander and I have something we are hoping to discuss with you."

Our boyfriend then looked straight at us, a steady glance from me to Zander, and I'd swear I saw "Oh, shit. What now?" in his eyes. "Say what?"

I couldn't help it. I reached over and took Zander's hand. He squeezed my palm, and I knew he was confused by Nate's attitude but still hopeful.

"Just listen to what Casey's gotta say, dude. It comes from both of us."

Those dark, distant eyes shifted again to focus on me. "'Kay."

And so I just let the babbler—who lived not too deep inside of me—out of his cage. I started flapping my gums like I was trying to fly away. "Well, you see, it's like this. The three of us, or 'us three' like you always say, well, we've been together for almost two years now, right?"

Nate nodded. I could feel the weight of Zander's stare pressing on the side of my face.

"And we are totally committed to each other. And dedicated too."

I got another nod from him, accompanied by an unspeakably confused look, but I pressed on. "We are in love, and like Zander said at the One Voice meeting last Sunday, we're a *family*."

Zander repeated my last words slowly and in a monotone, as if fascinated by them. "A family."

"And we wouldn't have discussed this whole thing without you, but it came up sort of suddenly. So we went ahead and talked about it and…."

I couldn't miss the stricken expression that passed across Nate's face. Evidently he was *afraid* of whatever we'd discussed when he was not in our presence.

"It's nothing bad, um… *sweetheart*." I threw that endearment in again for good measure, seeing as it seemed to capture his attention the first time I used it. "In fact, I think it's *good*."

"Just spill it." Nate's face, as well as his voice, were suddenly unreadable.

"Yes. Yes, okay. I can spill it." Zander squeezed my hand again, effectively letting me know he'd soon be taking the pressure off me, and I took a deep, relieved breath. "We want to move forward in our relationship. Like… um… like, sexually."

Those dark eyes popped open. "You wha—huh?"

"We wanna have sex, buddy. Us three. Together. You, me, and Casey. Next time you come down here." Zander finally contributed to the awkward discussion, spelling out what I was trying to gently introduce.

"You guys wanna g-get… uh… c-closer. As in—in the sack?" he asked.

Zander and I both nodded and then intentionally stayed quiet to give Nate a chance to absorb our declaration. Again Nate looked away, but this time he looked toward the floor and covered his face with his hands.

"So, are you into it?" Zander hadn't contributed much, but what he *had* said had been quite direct.

Nate, his hands still covering his face, spoke softly. "I ain't no virgin, ya know."

"What does that have to do with anything?" Zander was on a roll.

"Maybe you two should do each other the first time, ya get me? And I'll just watch. That'd be stellar."

"Fuck that," Zander replied in an even tone.

"But Zander, I been there. I done that. You two oughtta go for it first, and then *none* of us'll be virgins. It'll be equal 'tween us, you know? And maybe *then* we can do it, all three together. See?"

"Fuck that shit." Zander wasn't open to Nate's suggestion, and neither was I. "It'll be all of us in the bed or fucking none of us, dude. There's no reason why we can't do this. You've been tested, and you came out clean. And Casey and I haven't been with anybody else. We are all on 'equal ground' in that way, if that's what you're worrying about. Shit, man. We wanna make love together—*with you*."

Zander still held my hand, and his grip was so tight now that it hurt. I knew it was my turn to speak. I was the one who all of us expected to *say* the words—the one who expressed aloud what all three of us felt. "We love you. So much. We can hardly live without you here, and we want to be closer to you in every way. We want to share our bodies with you, Nate, and…." I had to take another deep breath to help me get through the sentence. "We want you to share your body with us. All of it." I couldn't help it. Instead of crying, I broke into a grin. The mental image was *that* good.

"Shit." Both of my partners were cursing like sailors now. "Ya know I love you guys too. I live for you two." When he lowered his hands from his face, I noticed his eyes had lost their faraway look, and I realized that maybe this awkward conversation had somehow connected us. I also noticed that his cheeks were quite pink, a new look for Nate. "Yeah. I wanna *get busy* with you guys. Fuckin' bad too. I wanna make you two mine in every way and…." His words trailed off, but soon he spoke again, his voice rough and gravelly. "Can't believe two guys like you want me like that. You know, in bed."

His honesty deserved reciprocal candor, so I said, "I want you and Zander *inside* me."

Zander released my hand and cupped the side of my face. But I was staring at Nate, taking in his surprise—his pleasure—at my words.

Zander said, "I want that too. Not too sure who's gonna do what to who, you know, but I want more intimacy with both of you."

We looked at the screen to see Nate's face as he issued his own confession. "Never had what I got with you guys, and I wanna show you how I feel with my body real fuckin' bad."

"It will happen the next time you come to visit. Okay, Nate?" I wanted to ask him to promise that we'd make love the next time we were together, and then I wanted to beg to see him that weekend so it could happen sooner rather than later, but that would only put more pressure on him to find a place for Cindy to stay.

Sometimes it felt like Zander and I were chasing an elusive minnow through a rushing stream. Every time we reached for Nate, he slipped right through our fingers.

Nate knew me well enough to anticipate my worries. "I promise, babe. Next time we're alone together, us three are gonna become one."

6
NATE'S DIARY

August 31

A FUCKIN' bad scene went down in our shit hole of a livin' room a little while ago. But me and Cindy, well, let's just say that Lady Luck was on our side. Cuz neither of us got the crap knocked outta us by Uncle Rich tonight.

First of all, my mood sucked, seein' as I couldn't find a place to leave Cindy for the weekend. Which meant no "us three becomin' one in the sack," to put it real polite. So, yeah, maybe I was pissed off, and maybe I didn't take to it real kind when Uncle Rich came home from work with a girl young enough to be his daughter (I knew the girl from high school, which made it so much fuckin' worse) and a plastic baggie filled with coke. I don't want that shit around me no more, and I sure as shit don't want it around Cindy. No fourteen-year-old needs to see that shit in her own home, and let me tell you, she was actin' real interested, which she mighta just done to piss me off. Which it did.

So I got right in the asshole's face, told him to take his bimbo and his bag of blow somewhere else. Bad idea. Me and Cindy ended up out in the truck, which is where we're sleepin' tonight. Cindy's already crashed. She bawled so friggin' hard about missin' some stupid-ass top modeling reality show on TV that she finally couldn't keep her swelled-up eyes open no more. Shoulda just took her to the truck before the big blowout went down, but I wasn't thinkin' too straight. Guess I got pissed off cuz I don't want my little sister gettin' into no drugs.

I sure gave Uncle Rich a piece of my mind, right in front of pretty Daria Willson. He looked at me cross-eyed, like he couldn't believe that I was in his face. And he kept shakin' his head cuz he couldn't believe his ears that I was cursin' him out. Didn't take long 'til them eyes turned into narrow slits in his face, and I knew I'd have hell to pay.

"Who you think you're talkin' to?" He musta said that five times before I found enough calmness inside me to answer the asswipe.

"Just don't think you oughtta be doin' no drugs with Cindy right here."

"I don't recall askin' for your opinion on the matter." That's what he came back at me with.

He pushed me hard, so I was up against the wall, and grabbed the neck of my T-shirt with both hands. I swear he woulda fuckin' killed me if Daria hadn't yawned and said, "You told me we were gonna do some coke, Richie, and I ain't here for my health, so...."

She was tellin' my asshole uncle that he didn't have time to beat on me. Pretty Daria was more than ready for her high, and it seemed that Uncle Rich was eager to indulge her. Looked like Daria from high school saved my sorry ass tonight.

Didn't have time to grab no blankets or nothin', but I had a couple sweatshirts in the truck, so I let Cindy curl up in 'em in the backseat. Found a T-shirt of Zander's under the driver's seat, so I stuck it under my head like a pillow and made do with that.

Last thing I'm doin' before I try and sleep tonight is writin' in my journal, cuz it helps to get my head screwed back on straight. Wicked lucky for me I was holdin' on to it when Daria and Uncle Rich came in the door. And right now I'm not as pissed off as I was before that I can't go and see my guys this weekend. Instead I'm just glad that me and Cindy are safe, even though we're safe in my truck and not in our beds. All I know is, there ain't no way I can leave Cindy alone overnight with Uncle Rich. She ain't got no restraint with her mouth, and he ain't got no restraint when it comes to his fists.

Her mouth and his fists add up to a hella bad combination.

So it totally sucks that I can't get my ass down to Boston, but it's a done deal. I'll probably text them two in the mornin' and let 'em know the crappy news.

ZANDER ZANE'S One Voice Blog Spot—by invite only

Your host, Zander Z

Yes. So I extended my first invitation to join the One Voice Blog Spot. Yeah—to you, Dan. Hehehe.

Here's a warm welcome to my big bro. You are my first official follower. Bet you never thought you'd see the day when you'd be an official follower of your baby brother. But that day has surely arrived. So remember, read carefully and leave comments at the end. Let's see if my brother knows how to follow simple directions. LOL.

Developing the One Voice group at BCC has taken up a good solid chunk of my time. It's probably taking away from the effort I dish out for schoolwork. And because of One Voice, I've decided not to play fall rec soccer. I told myself I'd join in the spring league instead. It's just that One Voice is my top priority. Casey calls it my obsession, but he always says it with this cute grin, so I know he isn't actually mad about it. I'm pretty sure Nate is 100 percent behind me too. But the guy has a whole bunch of other problems at home to deal with.

As it turns out, our partner, Nate, can't make it down to Boston to visit us this weekend. We had plans for our "throuple" for the weekend too. Big plans. "Epic" plans, as Casey calls them. Puzzle over that for a while, dude. On another note, I have homework to catch up on this weekend and Sunday's One Voice meeting to plan, so I was just starting to think maybe it wasn't so bad that Nate couldn't make it. But Casey helped me put it all in perspective. Here's how the conversation went down.

"I have an idea, Zander. How about we go home and visit my family for the weekend?" Casey was sitting at his desk, facing the wall, and I was parked on my bed, in the center of a ring of textbooks.

"So we can see Nate?"

"Well, yeah. He and Cindy can stay at my house too. We can all hang out together with my little sisters, and then Mom and Dad can go out to dinner for a date night," he said.

I know I shouldn't have done it, but I'm certain I hesitated so I could think this possibility through. "I don't know."

"Well, why not?" Casey ran his hand over his cropped blond hair. "What's more important than being together with Nate?" He can be damned persistent.

I still had to think about my answer a little bit more. "Well, to be what we want to be—as you call it, a 'throuple'—we need to have rights, as gay men and as sexually liberated adults. And if I don't take One Voice seriously, then it hurts our chances to reach those goals. Equal rights are not gonna just drop in our laps, Casey. Somebody has to fight for them."

Casey got up from his chair and came over to my bed. He sat down delicately beside the books and focused his gaze on mine. "One Voice is important." He didn't look away. "But we—your family—are *more* important."

It's funny how a single sentence of brief, to-the-point words can hit home way better than a long lecture ever could. I *felt* his words like an arrow to my heart. The fight I waged for One Voice is vital to me because it's personal. *It's because of the three of us.* I want to make a life with these two guys. I just want the life I make with them to be accepted and respected by the community. Casey had a point.

"You're right." I said it and meant it.

Casey's nose wrinkled when he smiled and it was so frigging cute. "I know." Then he broke into a grin. "Let's surprise Nate, okay?"

I nodded and took Casey into my arms. "I love you guys." When we say we love each other and Nate isn't there, we always tack the word *guys* to the end. We never let ourselves forget there are three of us.

"And I adore you guys, so let's make plans for how we can shock our sweet Nate on Friday night."

"Casey, we don't have to get back here Sunday night for the One Voice meeting either. I'll e-mail everybody and cancel it." Some things *are* more important.

But Casey surprised me. "There's no need to do that, Zander. We'll leave school right after class on Friday and plan to return on Sunday afternoon. Nate wouldn't want you to cancel the meeting. One Voice is part of what he loves about you. And part of why I'm emotionally strong today."

Dan, I know you are my sole audience member at this point. Plus I talk to you on the phone every other day, but I still want to point out what works so well in this relationship of mine, what validates its right to exist as much as anyone else's relationship. The three of us balance each other so perfectly. When I'm going overboard in a certain direction, then Casey brings me back. When Casey needs a feeling of physical strength beside him, he turns to Nate. When Nate needs to logically work out a problem with his sister or uncle or boss, he turns to me. And when we need to feel valuable and loved, we all turn to each other.

We are three. We are three guys. And we work together. We fit like puzzle pieces. I will not lose this precious love as I struggle to make society accept and embrace it.

I won't.

7
NATE'S DIARY

September 2

GOTTA HAND it to 'em, and Cindy too. They shocked the shit outta me. But in a good way.

I wasn't what you'd call pissed off at the world or nothin', but I was sure down and out. I was gonna have to spend my weekend alone here at home and not makin' love to my boyfriends. Shit. Maybe I was a little bit pissed off, but not at Cindy, more at the world. So on Friday at work, I was keepin' mostly to myself. Not hangin' in the garage 'tween customers to talk to the mechanics. Not chattin' with Missy, who works days at the minimart. Just coolin' my jets in the little hut 'tween the pumps.

So, at a quarter to six—when I was about to get off for the weekend—a black Volvo pulled up to the pumps. It was chock full of kids. When I took a closer look, Zander was drivin', and my little sister was in the passenger seat.

What the fuck?

I checked out the backseat, and there was Casey, sardined 'tween his twin sisters, Sarah and Lola. Three little blondies in a row. Super cute.

"Hi, Natey-Nate," Lola shouted out the open window.

"Fill her up, Mister Gas Station Man." Sarah had been coached. I could tell.

Zander popped outta the car and came around to where I stood by the pumps. He leaned over and gave me a quick hug before he opened the car's gas tank. I just stood there, starin' from Cindy to Casey, not sure what the fuck was up.

Casey wasn't one to keep quiet. "Nate, my mom needed gas, so she called up Zander and me, and asked us if we'd take her car to the gas station." He burst into laughter. "So we hopped on the train, made the two hour trip up here. Now here we are, doing Mom this little favor."

Pretty sure I was droolin' at that point, or at least my tongue was hangin' out. Cuz I didn't have a fuckin' clue how to react to what they done.

I felt Zander's hand on my lower back, pressin' just enough to remind me he was there. He spoke so soft into my ear. "We came home for the weekend, dude. All of us are staying at the Mintons' for the weekend."

"Me and Cindy too?"

Zander nodded. "Well, you *are* the reason we came home. Casey and me don't wanna spend a weekend without you if we don't have to."

And what came next, I couldn't believe. Zander got up on his toes and planted a soft kiss right, full on my lips. I fought the urge to look and see if the dudes workin' late in the garage were watchin' us. Not that I gave a shit, cuz the chills goin' up my arms and spreadin' across my chest felt so good.

Plus I lost my breath when I heard his words. It just meant so fuckin' much. "'Kay."

Cindy turned and glanced out the window. "Nate, if I get along good with the twins, Mrs. Minton said I could babysit them for real in the future." She was stoked.

"Mommy's making chenchy-wadas."

"Lola—it's enchy-wadas."

In the backseat, the girls started bickerin' over the way to say enchiladas. It didn't bother me at all, cuz I knew I was gonna be eatin' Mexican with my guys that night. And Cindy would be safe. And happy too.

"The guy who's on the pumps tonight is here, so lemme go and cash out. Then I'll stop by my house to get my shit, and I'll be right over."

"I already got your shit, bro. It's back at the Mintons' house, up in Casey's bedroom." My sister grinned like she was stoked that she pulled one over on me and then she hopped out of the Volvo. "I'll drive over to the Mintons' with ya, 'kay?" Cindy didn't wait for an answer. She just trotted over to the truck, and I thought maybe she was pumped up over us havin' a real family-like weekend.

I took the cash for the gas from Zander, who gave me a quick wink, and then I bent down to look into the backseat at Casey. "See ya in a few."

He smiled in that sweet way that only Casey knows how to do, and then they pulled away. I didn't waste no time gettin' my ass in the truck.

CASEY'S REAL LIFE

WHEN WE got to my house, my mother came and took the twins inside, and Zander and I waited in the driveway for Nate. I felt like a groom waiting for his bride. Except there were two grooms waiting for Nate, who was another groom. When Nate's truck finally pulled in, we managed to keep our cool until Cindy went inside. The second Nate came around the truck, though, we kind of attacked each other.

Zander and I pressed our bodies to either side of his chest, and I was only satisfied when I felt his arm come down around my shoulder.

"You guys. What the fuck're ya doin' here, huh?" Nate sounded dazed.

Zander replied quickly. "Our family comes first. The three of us being together is the most important thing."

I was glad that Zander had responded with such conviction. It proved to me that he understood what was truly important—that he had his priorities set correctly. I added, "We didn't want to be away from you for a weekend, and we figured, as long as we study while we're here, we can spend the weekend with our favorite people."

"I might have to take over nail-paintin' duties with your little sisters for ya, Casey. Y'know. So you can do your studyin'.'"

"You aren't going to have to be a manicurist this weekend." I couldn't help teasing him. "Your sister is staying with us too. She told me she loves painting nails. She even brought her own kit, with stickers and jewels. Lola and Sarah are going to be in manicure heaven."

"But wait, Zander." Nate pushed us both back. "You can't miss your One Voice meetin' on Sunday night."

Zander looked up at Nate's stricken face. I was pretty sure he realized, at that moment, just how important *his* goals were to Nate. Zander looked at me, his eyes wide and maybe a touch guilty. Then he spoke to Nate. "No worries, man, I'm not gonna miss the meeting. We'll leave Sunday afternoon in time to get to One Voice. Unless you want us to stay later, which won't be a problem. I can e-mail everybody and cancel, and I'll be glad to do it."

"No. No, Zander. I want you to get back for the meetin'. It's *important*."

Zander pulled his gaze from my face. "Not as important as *we* are."

Nate bent down and kissed Zander so sweetly I thought I might burst into happy tears. Even when Nate had ended the kiss, Zander kept his face lifted toward Nate, as if he were hoping for more. And when Nate bent down and kissed my lips, softly and reverently, I allowed a couple of isolated tears to fall from my eyes. Tears of joy were nothing to be ashamed of.

THE NIGHT was more than incredible. My mother's Mexican cooking is legendary, so we all ate until we had trouble fitting into our pants. After dinner, we climbed on the sectional couch in the family room—all of the "kids," Nate, Zander, Cindy, Lola, Sarah, and I, piled onto it with plenty of pillows and blankets. I had to give credit to my parents. They were incredibly accepting of what probably seemed a little bit strange to them—three guys in love.

They even made us popcorn and lemonade and then sat down together on the love seat in the far corner of the room. We all watched *Toy Story*. Though it was crowded on the couch, and stray little girl hands and feet kept finding their way to my ribs, I felt warm, cozy, and safe—part of a family. I hoped that Nate and Zander felt as connected and secure as I did.

WE SPENT much of Saturday in the same studying position as we spent most of senior year. I sat on the floor in front of the living room couch, where Zander and Nate sat close together. Nate kept his hand planted in my hair, which I'd missed. At dinnertime, Mom and Dad piled the girls in the Volvo and took them all to Dairy Queen for hot dogs and ice cream.

"I wanna take my guys out on the town." Once the crowd was out the door, Nate came to stand in front of Zander and me. "You guys been studyin' your asses off. Least I can do is feed ya good."

"But… but my parents took the g-girls out," I stammered. "That means we have a couple of hours *alone* before they go to their own dinner reservations."

I looked at Zander, who appeared extremely eager. Then I glanced back at Nate, who looked troubled. "No," was all he said before he turned toward the wall.

Zander and I exchanged confused glances, and then Zander said, "But I thought we were gonna… you know. I thought we were gonna *make love* next time we were alone."

Nate started shaking his head slowly.

"Why not?" My words sounded whiny. Nate just kept shaking his head, but I noticed that his shoulders had slumped down, making me want to hug him. So I went up behind him and wrapped my arms around his waist. "Why do you not want to make love to us?" I made sure to use a gentle tone.

Nate didn't turn around, but he did answer me. "I *do* wanna make love to you guys. More'n anything else." I could feel his chest swell against me as he took a deep breath. "It's just… I don't want it to happen here, *like this*."

Neither Zander nor I spoke. We knew that Nate had more to say, and sometimes he needed time to express himself. So we waited. "I don't wanna worry somebody's gonna come in and interrupt us. I don't wanna rush it. Don't wanna have to get up afterward, real quick, and throw our clothes on and act like nothin' super monumental just happened."

I understood his feelings, even if I didn't want to.

"After we get close like that, I wanna be able to hold you guys naked, like for hours."

Zander stepped up beside me, placed both hands on Nate's shoulders, and rubbed. "You're right. This isn't the right time."

Although I was disappointed, I also realized it was not our perfect moment. "So, Nate, where were you thinking of taking us for dinner? I've been seriously craving Japanese, if that helps you make a decision."

Nate turned around, his long arms still dangling awkwardly by his sides. "You guys get me? I mean, you get what I'm sayin'?"

We both nodded.

"I actually kinda love you more for what you just said, dude." Zander didn't make direct eye contact with Nate as he made this confession. "It's not all about sex with us. And you reminded us of that fact."

Nate blushed, his skin turning a deep red. He reached up, pulled his long hair off his shoulders, and held it against the back of his neck for a few seconds. "You guys are too special to rush it. But if we wanna get back from dinner before we have to babysit so your folks can go out, we'd better get our asses in gear."

I couldn't help it. I pretty much jumped on Nate. I wrapped my arms around his shoulders and my legs around his waist. "I love you guys so much. Our love is worth waiting for." I knew as I said it that I was going to buy candles and fancy glasses to drink fake champagne out of on the night we first made love. And that there would be mood music and satin sheets. Making love to these two men meant everything. The evening we became one would be perfect in every way.

8

NATE'S DIARY

September 8

DIDN'T GET off so easy last night. Had to call in sick to work today. Shit, I ain't sick. But I *am* a fuckin' mess. Can't be seen in public 'til the swellin' goes down some.

See, Cindy was in a nasty-ass mood last night. Like, what's new, right? She needed Uncle Rich's signature on some field trip permission slip and cash for her lunch account, and she wanted them things ASAP. Couldn't wait 'til Uncle Rich had sucked down a couple beers—enough booze to soften up his asshole mood. The girl seriously needed to stuff a sock in it, but no, she kept right on bitchin' at the man. And finally he'd had it. From where he was standin' in the kitchen by the fridge, he just turned around and chucked his empty beer bottle at Cindy, who was standin' in the hallway. Got her hard on the arm. She started wailin'. Before I knew it, he was goin' at her, his fists all balled up and ready to pound.

Couldn't friggin' let that happen.

I rushed in between them two. Knew I was gonna get the stuffin' beat outta me before I even moved. Did it anyhow.

Once Uncle Rich is in a rage, there ain't no coolin' down for him 'til he's pounded on somebody. I knew it had to be my ass that got whooped, not hers.

Only problem was, it wasn't my *ass* that took the brunt of the beatin'. Just so happened, my head was the closest thing to his raised fists. Beat on my ears and face 'til I crumpled up on the floor, coverin' up my head with my arms. Then he took a few good kicks at my belly for good measure, and he was out the door.

Thankfully, Cindy had the good sense to take off when he started clobberin' me.

I lay there for like half an hour or so after the beatin', I'd say. Breathin' fuckin' hurt. Movin' fuckin' hurt. Thinkin' even fuckin' hurt.

So I didn't call Zander and Casey last night and didn't answer their calls or texts or e-mails or nothin'. They just know me too well, and I was afraid they'd pick up that I was in total survivor mode. Needy as hell. One hurtin' unit. Then they'd leave school to come check up on me or some stupid shit like that. Can't have that happen.

This here is my problem.

Today I iced my face and sides 'til I thought I was gonna get frostbite. And I made myself accept that I wasn't gonna be able to see my guys this weekend. They'd take one look at me and put up a huge fuckin' fuss. Christ knows, I don't need that shit.

And Cindy, she'd have to be blind to miss that I'm one hurtin' unit, but she more or less pretends that she don't see it. She don't even make more ice for my injuries when she uses it all in her soda. It's like Cindy's testin' me to see how far she can push me before I take off on her too. Maybe she wants me to prove I love her enough to suffer for her. Don't really know her reasonin'.

My plan? Yeah, I got a plan. First off, gonna talk to Cindy about keepin' her trap shut when she's havin' an overload of teenage hormones. She don't need to make me prove nothin' cuz she oughtta know how much I care about her at this point. Second, just gonna tell my guys I have to work this weekend and I'll see 'em next weekend, for sure.

Easy enough, huh?

You'd think so. But my boyfriends are like pit bulls. They already called and texted me no less than ten times. "Where are you, dude?" "What's wrong, huh?"

Shit. They can't fuckin' find out. Don't know what they'd do or how they'd react to knowin' I got pummeled again. They wouldn't get that I'm *used* to this shit. *I know how to deal with this shit.* They'd want me to change things up—like for me to move

Cindy somewhere else and move down to Boston with them. But to me, and to Cindy too, changin' shit around seems like nothin' but a bunch of question marks for the future. Poor Cindy's had enough question marks. She needs to just stay put. At least I'm pretty sure that's what's best for her.

I know they wouldn't never get it, but here in NH, I got a place to live and a job, and I can look after Cindy some. Don't know what'd happen if things got changed up.

ZANDER ZANE'S One Voice Blog Spot—by invite only

Your host, Zander Z

Being in a relationship is complicated. Strange thing is, I don't mean being in a gay relationship, and I don't mean being in a throuple either. I guess every relationship has its difficulties, but the problem we're going through is mostly on account of our relationship's long-distance nature. Long-distance relationships can work—I'm fairly sure of that—but they require communication. And shit loads of it. When one of the participants is holding back, that's when the trouble starts.

And Nate is holding something back.

Last weekend was stellar. We stayed at Casey's house and ate great meals, watched movies, cuddled up on various soft, flat surfaces, and talked. And when Casey and I said good-bye to Nate, everything was damn close to being perfect between the three of us.

Monday was great. We texted each other love notes in all combinations—me to Nate and Nate to me, me to Casey and Casey to me, and Casey and Nate to each other. Tuesday—not a problem. We Skyped at night, and it was a freaking love fest.

The problem came on Wednesday. All of a sudden there was no Nate. Anywhere. It was as if he'd fucking dropped off the face of the earth. He didn't answer our phone calls, texts, or e-mails. He has no Facebook account, or we would have tried to message him there. So Casey went fucking nuts. And I had a damned bad feeling myself.

Thursday came—neither of us slept much Wednesday night—and he finally answered his phone.

"You're on speaker, dude," I said.

"Oh, megasorry about not answerin' your calls or nothin'," he said super casually, "but I wasn't feelin' great last night, and I dropped off to sleep right after work."

Like, yeah, right.

"How you guys been? Did you ace that bio exam, Casey? Aah, I'm sure ya did."

Our boyfriend was overly cheerful. Casey and I swapped eye rolls.

"And Zander, how're your One Voice plans for this Sunday comin' along, dude? Stellar, I'm sure."

Hello, we know you, Nate. We're not buying into this bullshit.

"By the way, guys. Gotta work this weekend, so I can't come down to Boston. Bummed as hell, but work is work, right?"

Tell me another one, dude.

"So, anyhow, can't talk too long. Gotta take Cindy to the mall. She says she needs a haircut, and who am I to argue with a teenage girl, huh?" His voice was like sweetness on steroids.

What the fuck is up with this?

Anybody who's reading this in the future—gay, straight, in a threesome or a foursome, or single even—listen carefully. You can't allow your partner or friend to bullshit you and get away with it. But—yes, there's a big but coming—but you have to choose your battles, select the right time to confront. Be tactful, yet get down to the heart of the matter. Casey and I knew it was *not* the right time. Nate was still dealing with whatever had him acting so fucked up.

Casey took the wheel. "Well, by all means, go take the girl for her haircut. Zander and I would never stand in the way of beauty."

Nate laughed, but the sound was forced and unconvincing.

"Sweetheart," Casey added. "We want to Skype you tonight. How's that sound?"

"Uh…," Nate uttered, and then silence.

"How's nine o'clock for you?" I asked, unwilling to give up.

"Shit, dude. Said I'd work at the Humane Society 'til late tonight. I'll… I'll text ya before bed."

"I want to *see* you." Casey was pushing and I was glad.

"Lookit. I'll Skype you guys tomorrow night after work, 'kay? Hey, gotta run. Cindy's chompin' at the bit to get to the salon."

And he hung up. Without saying "love ya" or "miss ya." He was just gone.

And for what seemed like the hundredth time in the past five minutes, Casey and I looked at each other and saw worry on each other's faces.

Danny. My man and my only brother—something's wrong. I know it. But I don't know what, and I don't know what to do either. Maybe your best advice should be sent to me in a text message or an e-mail. Maybe it's just too private for what will one day be a public forum.

CASEY'S REAL LIFE

I WAS so angry at him. I mean, probably it was one of the angriest, most frustrated, and helpless moments I'd experienced since I'd been humiliated by the girls on the soccer field that night my freshman year. And that's saying a lot. Because that night was hell.

Nate was lying to us. It was that simple. He skipped out on our phone call on Wednesday night, put us off on Thursday night, told us his Skype wasn't working right on Friday night, and was missing in action all day Saturday.

I felt like my blood was boiling. Something was wrong. *Really wrong.* And I didn't know what. Because of that, I didn't know how to go about fixing it. I didn't want Zander to see how upset I was, because I could tell he was having his own concerns about Nate. I didn't want to put more of a burden on his shoulders. So I hid myself away from him. I hid at the library, at the student cafeteria, at the student center. I actually even went to the recreational complex and attempted to run laps on the indoor track. Wonders never cease. I just needed to hide away from my feelings. And to hide from Zander, who knew me better than I knew myself.

On Saturday evening, I came home in time for our usual dinnertime text message from Nate. Unsurprisingly there was nothing from him. No text. No e-mail. No phone call. He'd blown us off again.

"This guy invited me to a party at his off-campus apartment. I want to go." It was true. A guy from my statistics class, Chad Hutchins, had invited me to his house party, probably to thank me for all the help I'd been giving him with organizing his notes each day after class. Anyone could see that Chad was a cool "player," and I was still Casey the nerd, so thankfulness or pity could be the only two options for this invitation.

"You wanna *party* tonight?" Zander appeared incredulous. Neither of us had indulged in alcoholic beverages in college.

"Yeah, but I want you to come too."

He nodded, a blank expression in his light brown eyes. I nodded back.

WE WENT to Chad Hutchins's party. I drank alcohol for the very first time in my life. I got "wasted," as Zander called it. We both did, I guess. After I threw up a couple of times off the back deck at the party, Zander said it was time that we called it a night.

My series of errors continued when we got back to our dorm room. After brushing the nasty taste out of my mouth and peeing for the zillionth time, I climbed into Zander's twin bed and started groping him. I was intentionally breaking the rules we'd set up with Nate. I was initiating sexual intimacy with Zander when Nate wasn't with us. And I was being pretty pushy about it.

I had my hand inside Zander's shorts when he gently pushed me away. "I know you're pissed off and hurt, Casey, but doing this isn't gonna make things any better with Nate."

That was all he had to say, and I started bawling like a two-year-old.

Zander held me tightly, and I knew he hadn't rejected me. He had just stopped me from doing something in a drunken fit of anger that would have devastated all three of us later.

"Why? Why didn't he call us? Is it over with us? Does he want to be free of you and me?" I cried and cried and questioned Nate's motives time and again.

Finally Zander leaned over to his bedside table and snapped on the light. Then he picked up his phone and started to dial.

"You can't call Nate now, Zander. It's two in the morning."

He ignored me and kept dialing. After a minute, he said softly, "Dude, it's me."

It appeared that Nate-the-absentee-boyfriend had been found.

"Yeah, something sure is fucking wrong with Casey." Zander listened to Nate for a few seconds before responding. "No, he's not physically injured. But he's drunk and losing it. He needs you." After a short silence, Zander added, "And I need you to level with us. So we're gonna Skype right now. Go get on your computer."

Just like that Zander got up off his bed and took his laptop from his desk. Within a couple minutes, Nate was on the computer screen. It was dark in Nate's bedroom. We could barely see him.

"Turn on the light, Nate."

Nate's shadow didn't move. "Don't wanna."

"Just do it." Zander's voice was calm but firm.

The shadow leaned over and turned on the light. And then Nate looked at us.

"Shit." Zander spoke first. I was too busy processing the array of bruises and cuts, swollen nose and puffy eyes to utter a sound. "Is this what happened to you Wednesday night?"

Nate nodded.

"You didn't tell us. You hid it from us like you don't trust us."

"I trust you guys." His voice sounded so tiny.

"Then why the fuck didn't you tell us what he did to you?"

Up until that point, only Zander had spoken to Nate, but I finally found my voice. "We would have come up to New Hampshire, taken you and Cindy out of there, called the police and children's services, and—"

"That's exactly why I didn't say nothin'."

I was stunned. "But—"

"Casey—I ain't figured all this shit out yet. Dunno why Cindy always riles up Uncle Rich so much that he *has* to beat on somebody's ass to get his head back on straight, and I know me and her gotta talk about it...." His eyes dropped to his bed or his floor. I wasn't sure. "And we gotta figure out if us two should make some kinda move from Uncle Rich's house. But just know I'm just so fuckin' sorry for givin' you guys the runaround." That was a lot for Nate to say all at once.

And there we sat. The two of us staring at our beaten boyfriend, knowing in our hearts how much worse it must have been on Wednesday night when it first happened. Because almost four days later, he looked horrible. His nose was swollen, as were both of his eyes, which were also blackened. There were what looked like scabbed-over scratch marks on his cheeks and his forehead. And this was just his face. God knew if his body was covered in more of the same.

"I'm sorry." He said it again and breathed very loud. My arms started aching to hold him. "I really do trust you guys."

Zander was still calm. "What the fuck happened?"

"He was gonna beat on my sister. I had to stop him." That pretty much told the whole story. A story we'd heard many times before.

"Did he beat up Cindy too?" Zander was getting the facts.

"Nah. He took it out on me instead."

Despite the fact that I knew how protective Nate was of Cindy, I asked, "Why does she persist on doing this to you? She knows how it's going to end. It's like she is trying to set you up for a beating."

Nate shrugged. "Uncle Rich did this to me, not Cindy."

To Nate's response, I said, "Well, you have got to get yourself *and* Cindy out of that situation. If you don't do it for yourself, Nate, understand that Rich *is* eventually going to get your sister alone, and God only knows what he'll do to her then."

"I just need a bit of time to figure this thing out, that's all," Nate mumbled.

"The next time he loses his cool could be too late." Zander was calm, but he was pushing the issue. "You and Cindy gotta talk about this whole living-situation thing sooner rather than later."

"But you guys know I don't never leave Cindy alone with him."

"You gotta take care of yourself too, man." Zander was insistent.

After another brief silence, Nate said, "I'll talk to her about it as soon as the time's right, 'kay?"

"Needs to be soon, dude." My partners were going back and forth on the subject.

So that's when I took over. "When we couldn't get in touch with you, I thought you wanted to leave us, Nate."

He chuckled, and it sounded much more like the Nate we knew. "That ain't never gonna happen, babe."

"I wish we were with you right now, so much." Intense relief washed over me.

"Far as I'm concerned, you guys *are* with me right now. Felt real alone before you called, but not no more."

"Nate, I just feel so dizzy, and my thoughts are a little jumbled up right now."

Again, the chuckle. "That's called *drunk*, Casey."

"I'll have Advil ready for him in the morning," Zander assured him.

"I'd say the kid's gonna need it."

And then I had to confess. "I tried to fool around with Zander tonight after we got back from the party. Nate, I was so mad, and I don't know just what came over me." I started to cry again, knowing that he was going to be hurt and angry, and it would probably be over for real between us because I'd acted so rashly.

But Nate just smiled. "We all do shit we aren't totally cool with when we're drinkin' *and* when we're freakin' out. No worries, Casey."

And what happened next was almost like a miracle. We just started talking. Zander always called this kind of chatting "shootin' the shit." I called it sharing our lives. We just talked about what had happened over the past few days when we'd been apart. The three of us talked until the sun came up.

Once again, we'd managed to work our way through a rough patch.

9

NATE'S DIARY

September 12

THEM TWO are good. But at being fuckin' sneaky—well, I'm better.

Put 'em off from Skypin' me 'til middle of the night, Saturday. By then my face was a whole fuck of a lot better than it had been earlier in the week, so them two didn't have to go through the fuckin' horror of seein' me bloody and *totally* mangled.

Thing is, they didn't know how bad it'd been. What they saw, three days after the fact, freaked 'em out. And guess I didn't end up avoidin' that little talk I been dreadin' about doin' something about our situation with Uncle Rich. But it didn't go as bad as I thought.

"Our situation with Uncle Rich" makes it sound like we're caught in some kind of an improper business dealin', where maybe he forgot to pay us for a job well done or some shit like that. But really, the situation is more like a fight for me and Cindy's lives. Don't know why, but I just can't make a sudden leap to change things. Guess I figure the devil I know already might be a whole fuckin' lot better than the devil I don't know. And maybe I known a lot of devils in my time.

At least with Cindy and me under the same roof, I got some control over what goes on with her. What if Cindy got stuck in a worse place and had nobody there to look out for her? I ain't gonna get no placement *with* her, seeing as I'm grown. She'd be on her own in foster care, and I just can't leave nothin' to chance when it comes to her. Cindy's pretty much the only real family I got to my name. Not too sure why she shoves me under the bus so much these days with Uncle Rich—alls I can guess is that this whole livin' with the devil thing ain't easy on her neither.

So anyhow, I put in my hours at the gas station today. Couldn't miss that the chill of fall was in the air neither. Seein' as I'll be workin' outside, pumpin' gas, I have a feelin' winter's gonna feel long and damn cold this year. But a job's a job, and cash is cash, so I'll do what's gotta be done. Gonna be outside walkin' the dogs at night too. As a matter of fact, I'll be headin' there right after I finish writin' this.

Us three are already gettin' our plans settled for this comin' weekend. Got the word from Aunt Terri that Cindy'll be welcome to come and stay, so I can bring her down after school and work are done on Friday and have a weekend with my guys.

So that three can become one, ya see.

Sounds kinda poetic, huh?

CASEY'S REAL LIFE

I ACED my bio exam just like Nate predicted. I just wished I was as good at real life interactions as I was with the study of organisms.

Tonight Zander and I were "double-dating" with two girls Zander knew from his ethics class who were also members of One Voice. I experienced severe anxiety at expanding my social circle from just Nate and Zander to include outsiders, and in particular, female outsiders. The events from high school—the humiliation of freshman year, the emotional abuse and bullying, the physical assault in junior year—had left me with scars. Thick, deep, ugly purple scars on my heart. The wounds had healed over but the scars had never disappeared.

I just wished it were Friday and I was holding hands with Zander in the student center parking lot, waiting for Nate to arrive, dreaming of making love and of waking up in the safety of my lovers' arms. But no. Instead I was sitting stiffly beside Zander in the student-run fancy restaurant, the Hawk's Key, both of us dressed up in khakis and button-down shirts, awaiting the arrival of two teenage girls.

I'm not gonna lie. I felt the beginnings of a panic attack coming on.

"You don't look too good, Casey. Everything cool?" Zander asked, his brow wrinkled with worry.

I nodded and reached for my glass of ice water.

"You're gonna love these two girls. Just give them a chance, for me." Zander wanted me to open up my heart to new people.

Give them a chance, Casey. The words swirled around in my brain. The problem was, I remembered giving some girls a second chance in high school, and I ended up in the hospital.

"Here they are." Zander slid out of the booth to greet two young women who were heading across the restaurant in our direction. I concentrated on not fainting.

The smiling girls each hugged Zander. One of them was tall and very sporty looking—immediately and alarmingly bringing to mind Marcy Lewis from high school, a girl who had been one of my major tormentors. I couldn't stifle a shudder when I remembered Marcy swatting my butt with her high tops on the soccer field freshman year. The other girl was small, pixie-like, black, and just about as cute as a button. Like Liz Trainer, the ringleader of the high school bullies. The cute ones always spelled the most danger. My chest constricted uncomfortably.

"You guys know my boyfriend, Casey, from One Voice. Casey, this is Anna"—he indicated the Marcy look-alike—"and Claire." The too-adorable-to-be-kind one.

They slid into the booth across from where I sat, and Zander rejoined me, immediately placing his hand on my knee.

Anna extended her hand across the table, and I feebly reached out to take it in mine. "Oh, Casey, it is so great to have a chance to get to know you on a more personal basis than we can at One Voice."

Her green eyes sparkled with what appeared to be genuine warmth. But for me, it was hard to trust.

I took a controlled breath and blew it out. "Thank you. Glad to get to know you too." I wondered if it was obvious that I was lying.

Claire had to sit on her feet in order to reach my hand. "I'm super thrilled to meet you, Casey. I just wish your other partner, Nate, could be here too. It feels like somebody's missing."

What she said demonstrated her open-mindedness to our throuple. The muscles binding my chest loosened up slightly.

"Casey, Anna and Claire were high school sweethearts, just like me and you and Nate." Zander squeezed my knee. He knew how hard this was for me, but he also knew I needed to be able to interact socially with people besides Nate and him, especially if I wanted a future in medicine.

"High school bit the big one," Anna pronounced bluntly. "We had to hide our relationship for three years."

Claire looked at her girlfriend with unmistakable warmth. "We promised each other that there would be no more hiding in college, so now we don't hide at all. That's why we were so happy to see the signs for One Voice in the student center. It's extremely necessary."

For a moment, it was almost as if Zander and I weren't there with them. Anna reached her arms around Claire. "I wish we had had a gay-straight alliance like One Voice in high school. Everything would have been different."

"Things would have been better." The two young women were momentarily lost in each other's eyes. Seeing that, my dry mouth moistened a little bit.

We went on to discuss our majors—Anna and Claire were both enrolled in the School of Social Work at BCC—and our personal goals as members of One Voice. By the end of the dinner, I had confessed to these two girls that I'd had a very difficult time in high school. I didn't go into great detail about the bullying I suffered. I avoided opening that can of worms, but I think they got the general picture. And Claire had shared how both of them had hidden deep in the closet, occasionally even dating boys to keep up the charade, terrified right up until their graduation day that their peers would discover their love. They had attended a Christian high school, where they knew their relationship would have been frowned upon, to put it mildly.

"So your partner, Nate, is coming down for the weekend?" Anna smiled. "Maybe we could all have dinner together at the student caf' before the meeting?"

Zander returned the smile. "That sounds great." He winked at me. "If I decide to let the two of them out of bed."

Knowing our intimate plans for this weekend, I felt a furious blush climb up my neck and make itself at home on my cheeks. I giggled.

"Well, I can't say that I blame you one bit." Claire also winked at me. "You three haven't been together in a couple of weeks, right? You'll need plenty of time to get reacquainted."

I think I blushed even brighter.

I felt as if I had accomplished something by surviving and even enjoying the evening with two teenage girls. *With friends.*

10
NATE'S DIARY

September 19

I DON'T know just when this journal became so friggin' necessary to me. But it's like, after any major shit goes down, I can't get to this notebook fast enough to write about it, just so I can read it back to myself and make some sense of my life. Yeah, fucked up. But fucked up in the good way, I'd say.

Today I'm gonna write about the most amazin' weekend of my life. And no, I ain't shittin' nobody here. The weekend was awesome. Wish it never had to end.

SO ON Friday, I dropped Cindy off at dinnertime, and she seemed pretty pumped to be with Aunt Terri and Jana. That was a good feelin'. I didn't have to worry my ass off about Cindy bein' pissed at me cuz I dumped her somewhere.

When I got to Boston City College, my guys were waitin' for me in the parkin' lot, same as last time. It was kinda fucked up, though, cuz we all knew what was gonna happen 'tween us three this weekend, and maybe even that night. It was sort of awkward, but not in a bad way. Casey was a little shy when he greeted me. There wasn't no jumpin' into my arms and wrappin' his legs around me or nothin'. And when me and Zander's eyes met, it was like we both had a secret we was keepin'. Truthfully we were almost a little more like strangers than boyfriends for goin' on two years.

I could feel their eyes studyin' all of the healin'-up yellowish brown bruises and scabs on my face. And I could practically hear their thoughts about how pissed off they were at my uncle for smackin' me around, but they didn't say nothin' about it right then. Guess they knew me well enough to let it pass by for the moment. Complainin' about my asshole of an uncle wasn't exactly friendly to the electric, romantic mood we had goin' on.

Casey made us wait a few minutes in the parkin' lot while he ran back to the dorm ahead of us. He said he had to get shit ready. Well, he didn't actually say "get shit ready." He more said something like "I must make some vital preparations." You know, "get shit ready" in Casey language.

So me and Zander shot the shit in the parkin' lot for, like, ten minutes before we slowly walked back. Wanted so fuckin' bad to wrap my arm around his waist as we walked, but without Casey, our "glue," I felt too friggin' awkward. What made me fuckin' psyched was that, about halfway up to the dorm, Zander grabbed my bag offa my shoulder, took my hand in his, and squeezed—so I'd know we was together and on the same page and shit.

Casey texted Zander and asked him to knock on the door to their room when we got there, instead of using his key. So Zander knocked kinda soft. When Casey opened the door, his face was that certain shade of pink that made me worry he might have one of them panic-attack thingies.

So we went in the room, and what I saw pretty much melted me. Casey had gone to trouble, big time, to make this night special. The beds had already got pushed together, and they were covered in shiny red sheets. On Zander's desk, there was this plate with like a dozen humongous strawberries that'd got dipped in chocolate. Over on Casey's desk were these fancy-ass glasses filled with a bubbly drink. I saw a half-empty bottle of cranberry ginger ale on Casey's bureau, so I was pretty sure the glasses weren't filled with booze. He had some music playin' nice and soft too. It was U2's "One Love." Friggin' love that song.

Our sweet Casey had set the scene just perfect for our first night of love, when us three would become one.

WITHIN A few minutes, the three of us was stretched out on them slippery red sheets and naked as the day we were born. And I was nervous as all hell, seein' as I was supposed to be the sex expert. I was the only one who'd ever done the deed before. But let me get somethin' straight. Sure, I'd fucked a girl or two in the past. But it was *way* friggin' far in the past, I couldn't hardly remember any details cuz I'd been drunk or stoned when I done it, plus it hadn't meant nothin' to me, cuz them girls hadn't meant nothin' to me.

This here sex was gonna be so different. As in, the fuckin' opposite of all that.

This here was lovemakin'. With two dudes I friggin' couldn't live without.

Yeah, this was different as night was from day.

LUCKY FOR me, Casey wasn't bein' shy no more, the way he'd been earlier in the parkin' lot. He climbed right on top of me, his little body squigglin' around up there, like he was tryin' to feel up my whole naked body with his. And two seconds later, he was crawlin' onto Zander, doin' the same adorable shit. Me and Zander just looked at each other, like, "holy crap," cuz it felt so good.

Took us two a couple minutes to settle him down, cuz the little dude was all pumped up. So after he went back and forth, humpin' on us each a couple times, we sorta stuck him 'tween us so he was lyin' down flat on his back, and both of us leaned over him. I took that moment to kiss Zander supergood. From the way his tongue poked out real far into my mouth, I could tell he was ready to go. We didn't rush the kiss neither. I took my time explorin' the shit outta his mouth. He tasted so good, like the strawberries we'd just sucked down.

We kept kissin' 'til we heard this soft moan from underneath us, which was Casey, wantin' in on the action. In a split second, us two were on him. I went straight for that soft spot behind his ear, and Zander moved his mouth around on Casey's lips.

It was weird bein' this fuckin' turned on at the same time as bein' so much in love. Like wantin' to get what my body needed so fiercely, but just as much needin' to make it good for them two. I had to slow myself down more than once.

I let my lips slide down onto Casey's neck, where his pulse pounded like a friggin' bass drum, and then onto his tiny nipples. Once I started suckin' and Zander joined me on his other side, Casey got kinda outta control. My plan was to go down on each of my guys' dicks, you know, before we got to the main attraction. But I could see that the main attraction was gonna have to be the *only* attraction, at least this time around.

"Who's gonna do what to who?" I was super glad Zander asked so I didn't have to.

Casey didn't answer. He just squirmed and moaned. That left me to do the answerin'. "How about we get Casey ready together, and then you make love to him. Y'know, you make love to his back door, and I'll take care of his front door with my hand?"

I looked at Zander, who was starin' across Casey's chest at me, and he nodded. I couldn't miss that he was pantin' too. Guess that made three of us.

"Night table… drawer…," Casey uttered. "Lubricant."

I reached over and pulled open the drawer. Just like Casey said, I found a brand new bottle of lube. "No condoms?"

"We're virgins." That came from Zander. "And you been tested. You're clean."

Holy shit.

That was when Casey turned onto his belly in a clear invitation. Again I looked at Zander, but his eyes were locked onto Casey's smooth white butt. So we took turns squirtin' lube on each other's fingers, and then we went to work.

Never touched nobody back there, and it was sure different, but it was also real good. What was fuckin' great, though, was watchin' Casey's reaction to our finger invasion. Fuck, that dude was in what I'd call heaven on earth. Like he'd been waitin' all his life to be loved like this. By us two, of course.

"Put some lube on your dick." Somebody was bound to explode if we didn't get this show on the road ASAP. Real quick, Zander did as I suggested. "Now I'll hold him and kiss him and stroke him while you get inside him, 'kay?"

Zander made a squeakin' sound and then nodded.

And that's how it went down. We rolled Casey onto his side facin' me, and Zander snuggled up behind him, closed his eyes, and pushed his way inside real careful. I held Casey right against my chest, rubbed on Zander's arms, watched both of their faces for signs of pleasure and pain, reached one hand down, and stroked Casey's dick.

I had meant to kiss Casey while Zander was lovin' on him, but truth be told, I couldn't stop starin' at the beauty of my lovers. Zander's eyes stayed closed tight for the longest time, until he finally cracked 'em open and gazed at me. His eyes were glassy with both pleasure and strong emotion, I'd say. And Casey whimpered a bit as Zander made his way inside. He stared up at me with so much trust and love in his eyes I wanted to friggin' cry. And once Zander'd got goin' in a regular pattern of thrusts, I matched up my strokes on Casey's dick, as best I could. Soon both of my lovers were starin' up at me, wearin' the same glassy-eyed gazes of love and the most intense pleasure they ever knew.

And I was satisfied. Seein' my guys like that was all I ever really wanted or needed in the world. As they got close to comin', both of them clung onto me—Casey to my chest and Zander to my arms—like I was their port in a storm. I took that moment to tell them what they needed to hear and what I needed to say.

"I love you guys for always. Never gonna be apart. Love my strong Zander. Love my sweet Casey. Us three together. Us three are one now."

And pretty much at the very same moment, those two started comin'. I knew cuz of the way they shuddered and groaned and their eyes rolled back. A friggin' stellar sight to see is what it was.

Swear to God, it wasn't a half a minute before them two were goin' down on me—both of 'em at once. They just kinda pushed me onto my back and dove onto me. Soon they were lickin' and suckin' me like there wasn't gonna be no tomorrow. Felt so good, I can't start to explain it.

When I finally let go and shot, one of 'em was suckin' me and one of 'em was murmurin' words of how much they both loved me right against the inside of my thigh. Couldn't say who was doin' which thing to me. Didn't know. Didn't care. Cuz it didn't much matter, did it?

When the storm was over, them two lay down on the sides of me, and I wrapped an arm around each of 'em. Couldn't think of no words that were suitable for the moment, so I stayed quiet.

"Shit." That was what Zander came up with to say, which is probably what I woulda said.

"Want some ginger ale? We can toast our love and drink it out of those fancy glasses. I got them downtown at the Crate and Barrel with this very moment in mind and…."

Yup. Looked like Casey was back to chatterin' again.

I was just so fuckin' happy. I felt complete for the first time in my life—as in, complete in every way. And I knew that nothin' was ever gonna change this for us three.

THE TRUTH? Well, if I can't tell it here, there ain't no place I can tell it.

I didn't really want to go anywhere for dinner. Woulda been happy just orderin' in—pizza or Chinese or somethin'—so we could've stayed right there, naked in those shiny red sheets. But Casey and Zander had somethin' else on their mind for dinner, and along with dinner, a serious conversation about "your situation with Uncle Rich." Yup, there it was again.

They took me to a local Italian place, which wasn't too fancy or nothin' but was busy—the kinda place that if somebody was lecturin' you about somethin' or other, you'd have to just sit there and listen to him unless you were willin' to make a scene. Which is pretty much exactly what happened to me.

"How is your ravioli, Nate?" Casey asked.

"The sauce is a little spicy, huh, dude?" Zander said.

That was how them two got it started—with questions about my pasta.

Real quick, though, they moved on to tougher-to-talk-about shit.

"Your face is really a mess, dude. That asshole pummeled you." Zander went first this time.

But Casey jumped on the bandwagon real fast. "And your chest, Nate. Your chest—well your stomach, more. He kicked you there, didn't he?"

I sighed real loud. "Why're you guys askin' me this? It won't change nothin'."

Zander pushed his half-eaten plate of lasagna to the middle of the table. "It won't change things? Shit, Nate, the fact that he beat your face 'til he busted your nose and blackened your eyes and that he kicked you in the belly hard enough to break your ribs won't change where you're living and who you're living with?"

For a minute I thought Zander might get up and leave. He seemed real disgusted with me. He couldn't even bring himself to look at me for a good long while after he asked me that. I fought the feelin' of regret that I'd let Casey and him down. Cuz Casey looked every bit as messed up about this subject as Zander.

"We're afraid that he…. Listen, Nate, your uncle loses control—completely. Someday he could hurt you or Cindy very badly." Casey was tryin' so hard to get me to see it his way.

"I don't never leave Cindy alone with him."

My boyfriends glanced at each other, and then Zander said, "Well, *you* matter too, Nate. Cindy pisses Rich off, and then you take the beating for it. Can't you see that, dude? You gotta get out of there, man."

Casey actually got up outta his seat and came over to my chair. Then he knelt down on the carpeted floor right beside me and took my hand. And yeah, the other people eatin' there were watchin' us like we were some kinda dinner show, but I didn't give a shit. "I know how hard it is to make changes in your life, Nate. You watched me struggle with making a change junior year in high school, and you still see me struggling, to this very day, not to be scared of the world. Please listen to us and make some changes before you have to pay a heavy price like I did." He brought my hand to his lips and kissed my skin softly and slowly, almost like he worshipped me. "Think about this, Nate, for Zander and me, but mostly for Cindy and you. Think about reporting this abuse to the police and getting out of there." He reached up and ran his fingers over the scabs on my cheek, a supersad look on his face, and I knew he wasn't playin'. He *really* believed we were in danger. He was probably right.

"And just saying, Nate, Cindy is getting into a bad pattern of behavior. She's doing whatever she can to piss off your uncle and set you up to get your ass kicked. You know we love your sister, but there's some serious anger going on in her to treat you like that. She needs help, as in, to talk to a psychologist or something." Zander seemed to be offerin' the guidance counselor's viewpoint.

I could see what they were sayin' but I just needed some more time to think it all through.

"I'll think on it, 'kay?" I stood up and lifted Casey onto his feet. He shouldn't be kneelin' at nobody's feet, especially not mine. "I'll think on it real hard."

Zander took that moment to stand up too. So us three were standin' in the middle of the Italian restaurant, gapin' at each other.

And Zander told me, "You aren't replaceable to us, man. We love you and we need you. We don't have anything without you. So promise us you'll think about this situation soon."

I swear to Christ that his brown eyes got all filled with tears—over me. Over the big, dumb oaf, burnout loser, Nate DeMarco.

And then Casey, tears actually spillin' over onto his cheeks, spoke in this choked-up voice, "Promise us."

What else could I do, huh? I nodded.

But Casey spoke up again. "That's not enough. Promise it in words."

So I looked from Casey to Zander, and then I closed my eyes and promised. "I promise I'll think real hard when I go home this week, 'kay?" My partners had been holdin' on to the air in their lungs 'til I promised out loud, and they'd finally let all of that air inside 'em go. "Now, sit on back down and finish eatin'. You two're gonna need your energy for what I got in mind for us three tonight."

We all turned red. But we sat down and ate real quick.

CASEY'S REAL LIFE

WHEN I lost my innocence—my virginity—last weekend, I didn't "lose" anything at all. I gained two more parts of me—two more hearts to bond with, two more bodies to share, and two more minds to learn and explore.

Friday night was actually the night when we all made love for the first time, but the act wasn't complete until Saturday night. By Sunday morning, we had all become each other's, in every sense.

Saturday night was amazing. Like three eager puppies on our way to the food bowl, we rushed back to our dorm room after our Italian dinner. We couldn't wait to bond with our bodies, enhancing the love we shared in our hearts. Once we were through the door, I was pulling off my clothes and at the same time trying to help Nate yank off his boots and jeans. I'm sure I looked comical as I tore open my button-down shirt, then bent to tug at Nate's work boots, then squirmed around to lower my pants without the extra effort of unbuttoning and unzipping, and finally fell over in an effort to get my hands on Nate's fly.

Meanwhile, Zander had sauntered over, as if he were really casual about *Making Love Part Two*, and was playing music on his iPod.

"Cool, Bob Marley," Nate said. "One Love." Nate was always really tuned in to music.

There was definitely a musical theme of "one" going on in this room for those few nights, and I approved wholeheartedly. "Come on over here, Zander," I squeaked, needing my other man so badly.

When Zander finally got close to the bed, Nate and I were already naked, so both of us focused on him. I reached over, grabbed the hem of his T-shirt, and pulled it over his head in a single rather adept motion, like I'd been practicing. And then Nate massaged Zander's crotch, crooning softly. He was bent over slightly, so his lips were at Zander's ears. I couldn't make out exactly what Nate was saying, but I could tell from Zander's expression that he liked it.

Then Nate began to work on the button and fly of Zander's jeans with his big hands. He proclaimed in a stronger voice, "I wanna make you both mine tonight."

After he said that, Zander shuddered—about a second before I shuddered. I knew tonight was going to complete our physical connection.

The make-out session that followed was the most intense we'd ever known. We flung our bodies on the bed and went crazy. While Nate and I kissed, Zander put his face close to ours and whispered, "Let him in, Casey. Open your mouth wide for Nate."

When Zander kissed me, Nate watched and said, "So fuckin' beautiful. So fuckin' perfect, you two are."

When I saw Nate taking Zander's lips like they were the last bit of nourishment on the face of the earth, I said, "We love each other. We will forever. The three of us will be together always."

We even did a three-way kiss, which featured our tongues poking out as far as we could manage so they could all tangle together. It was nothing less than exhilarating. But we all ended up with very wet chins.

By the time we started touching each other, we were about as excited as three guys could get. But we still didn't rush things. They put me between them, like they usually do, and started by running their hands all over my body. I felt like a spoiled cat getting petted by two loving humans. I reciprocated as much as I could, reaching out to touch their chests and faces—just light brushes with my fingertips, between gasps I couldn't hold back.

"Let's get him ready." Zander spoke first. Then just like the night before, Nate grabbed the lubricant out of the drawer, and they squirted each other's fingers.

Nate said very seriously, "It's time to flip over onto your belly."

I heard an echo in my head of female voices saying close to those same words four years before. In fact, just about *exactly* four years ago. But this was so different. The loving tenderness, reverence even, they showed me washed away the fear, the humiliation, and the suffering of that assault. These two men loved me, and I would willingly turn over, expose my backside to them, so they could further demonstrate their love.

Once I was on my stomach, several warm fingers invaded me, while others rubbed my thighs and the flesh of my rear end. I wasn't sure who was doing what back there.

"Get up on your knees, Casey," Zander encouraged me.

Although I was trembling from excitement, I did as he said.

Nate got right behind me, and he spoke. "Open up your legs just a bit, babe."

I lowered my head to the bed and spread my legs enough to give Nate the access he needed. As Nate pushed inside, Zander stretched out beside me, leaned up and covered my lips with his, and swallowed all of my gasps. Soon Nate was moving in and out of me in a steady rhythm. Every once in a while I felt an electric spark of sensation that elevated my sensitivity ten notches. When I started panting into Zander's mouth, he reached beneath me and began stroking. With the feeling of both my men loving me at the very same time, I couldn't hold back, and I let myself go into Zander's hand.

Nate pulled out of me, bent down, and kissed the back of my neck as I slowly returned to earth. Once I trusted my voice to work again, I said simply, "Zander's turn." Nate wiped himself off with a towel I'd put beside the bed.

Zander was what you might call eager. He flipped onto his belly, and Nate and I adjusted our positions so he was between us. Nate, I noticed, was still very excited, as he hadn't climaxed when he made love to me. The two of us prepared Zander's backside with more lubricant and more touching. When Zander started to moan softly, I felt a tenderness and connection to him I had never before experienced. Zander, so cool and calm, was lying on his stomach, showing us his vulnerability. It was beautiful and precious, and Nate and I looked at each other and smiled.

"You wanna take him, Casey?" Nate was still looking at me.

For a few seconds, time stood still. I knew for a fact that I didn't want to do that. I didn't want to be on top of him. I didn't want to push my way inside Zander or Nate, but I also didn't have the words to explain my feelings. I had this inner knowledge of myself and what I wanted sexually. And I didn't want to do that.

I shook my head, and Nate nodded.

"It's okay, babe. You do what you wanna do. *Just* what you wanna do." I watched as Nate positioned Zander and gradually entered him.

For a full minute, I just watched Nate's expression of concerned tenderness, combined with controlled pleasure, as he studied the flexing of the muscles in Zander's back. I saw Zander squinting and rolling back his eyes as he adjusted to the loving invasion—wanting it and enduring it, both at the same time. And what I saw wasn't dirty or shameful or pornographic. Not even slightly. It was the picture of beauty. The picture of trust.

I saw my future on that bed beside me.

Zander pulled me toward him so I would share in the moment. At almost the same time, Nate grasped my shoulder and drew me against his thigh. So I joined them. I leaned up and kissed Nate deeply as he made love to our Zander. Next I flattened myself on the bed on my back close beside Zander, and I did as he had for me. With my lubricated hands, I grabbed his penis and tugged at it in time with Nate's thrusts.

"Kiss me, Casey. Please… I wanna be kissing you when I come."

I stretched up, parted Zander's lips with my tongue, and explored the inside of his mouth as he pushed himself into my hand. Soon Nate's movements became frenzied. Before I knew it, both of my lovers were grunting and then groaning. I recognized the sounds as those of both physical satisfaction and emotional fulfillment.

When it was over, I snatched up the towel beside us on the bed and cleaned my lovers. Then they cleaned me.

"You didn't get inside me, Zander." Nate looked almost guilty.

Zander and I both looked at Nate, but Zander was the one to respond. "We have the rest of our lives for me to get inside you." He said it with such confidence, such sureness, that his words caused goose bumps to rise on my arms and chest. The smile that spread across Nate's face—and I mean, it lit up his whole face—made Nate appear more stunningly beautiful than ever before. Then Zander added, "And Casey, you haven't topped either of us."

"I don't want to." If I couldn't be honest with these two men, I couldn't be honest with anyone. "It's just not... not me."

Both men nodded, accepting my decision easily.

"If ya change ya mind, just scream," Nate instructed me with an adorable directness.

Zander and I smiled at Nate.

"You guys will be the first to know if I change my mind."

Zander yawned and sort of pushed me and then Nate onto our backs. I knew he was tired and ready to sleep. Like always, I ended up in the middle, and both of my lovers crowded in on me. I stayed on my back, and they faced me on their sides, curled against me, our feet tangled together in a way that I loved.

"I love you guys." It was all I could think of to say. It sounded so good, we let it ring in the darkened room as the last words of the night.

ZANDER ZANE'S One Voice Blog Spot—by invite only

Your host, Zander Z

***Note to self*—remove before setting blog to public

This is a private post. Dan, since you're my only follower right now, I'll post it here. But before I let the public read my blog, I'm gonna take this one down. Too personal.

So yeah, dude, this post is gonna be like the old days back in high school when I sent you all of those TMI e-mails. And this one is gonna live up to the old "TMI way." Enjoy if you can get through it without too much "ewwww." LOL.

You are talking to your now nonvirgin little brother. Yup. You heard me right. Nate came for the weekend. And we "did the dirty deed" several times over. And there was *nothing* dirty about it. I am so glad we waited 'til we were older and out of high school—*really* ready—and that we waited to make love until a day when we had time to spend alone with each other before, during, and after the big moment. You know?

I just love those two guys so much. I know I'm only eighteen, but I see a real future with them. It's like we fit, just the way you and Abby do. It's real. Incredibly real. And I need you to understand that. I need you to respect our relationship and to accept it as much as I accept your relationship with Abby. You've never said anything to me to lead me to believe that you have a problem with the three of us being together. But not saying anything negative is not enough, Dan. I want you to love Nate and Casey as if they were two more brothers. The way I love Abby like a sister.

I feel relieved that I just put this all out there for you to read. It's been on my mind for a while now, and writing it here will give you a chance to read it and then think it over. Maybe you can call me over the next few nights, and we can talk.

OKAY, SO back to One Voice business. For reasons that I'm sure you can figure out from reading what I've written so far in this post, I am more committed to One Voice than ever before. On Sunday, all three of us attended the One Voice meeting, and it felt so right. But first let me tell you about how we met up with these two girls from One Voice, Anna and Claire, for dinner.

Anna and Claire are a lesbian couple I met in my ethics class. I invited them to join One Voice right off the bat. They have a few things in common with Casey, Nate, and me. That might sound weird, as they are a lesbian couple and we are a gay threesome, but they do. They were high school sweethearts like we were. And they had to hide the truth of their relationship for fear of the reaction of the other students at their Christian academy. And like them, we also kept our relationship quiet until the very end of high school.

Anna and Claire are really committed to One Voice. They haven't missed a meeting. Early last week I introduced Casey to them. I thought he was gonna have a panic attack, as he and teenage girls make for a tough combination, but he ended up liking them. I was proud of him. He forced himself to give them a chance, and it turned out so cool.

BTW, I was completely up front with the One Voice group that I was involved in a threesome, or as Casey calls it, a throuple. After the group members stared at me for a few seconds, all but one just accepted it. This one dude proclaimed we were all fucked up and took off. But I figure, nobody should give a flying fuck what I do in my bed, right? So anyway, Anna and Claire suggested that the three of us meet them for dinner before the One Voice meeting on Sunday evening.

We met up at the student caf' on lower campus, where we'd never eaten before. The girls wanted to try it out, as it has a new stir-fry station. I could tell Nate didn't want to go. He hinted around about leaving before dinner and getting on the road to pick up his sister, but I refused to let him off the hook. Casey and I have high hopes that he'll be joining us in Boston sooner rather than later, and it's important that he feels he's part of our life here. Having mutual friends is an important part of that.

So off we trudged. It was a twenty-minute walk from upper campus to New Caf, which is what everybody calls it. Nate, of course, was silent, and Casey wasn't his usual chatterbox self, probably because of his inner mistrust of teenage girls and his sadness that Nate would be leaving that night.

The girls were waiting for us when we got there, and they were as bubbly and sweet as always. I could tell they were working hard to put Nate at ease.

"So, Nate, we meet again." Anna was the first to speak. "Do you remember us from the One Voice meeting you attended a few weeks ago? I'm Anna, and this is my girlfriend, Claire."

Nate nodded and grunted something affirmative.

The two girls smiled widely at Casey too. I noticed that his shoulders relaxed, probably from relief at their overt friendliness.

"This new stir-fry bar is supposed to be awesome. We've been dying to try it."

We followed Anna as she headed to the food services area.

Once we were all seated in front of plates of stir-fried rice and vegetables at a spacious circular table, a conversation between the five of us finally got going, and I was able to relax.

"So where do you work, Nate?" Anna immediately took charge of the conversation. That's kinda her style.

"I… uh… I just pump gas." Nate didn't remove his eyes from his rice.

"Well, I pumped gas at a marina near my house every summer since I was fourteen. And it's paying for all of my room and board here at BCC. So I have pumping gas to thank for this very forkful of chicken, rice, and bean sprouts." She smiled and shoveled it into her mouth.

Nate looked up at her. "I walk dogs too."

That's when Claire chimed in. "My mom is a dog groomer. I've been the official dog walker for her business for about as long as I can remember."

Claire got a tentative smile from Nate.

"Have you ever seen one of those tiny papillons? They're so cute," Claire said.

"Um, I walk dogs at an animal shelter—mostly mutts."

And so ensued a conversation about mixed dog breeds.

Casey wasn't babbling away, but he appeared relaxed and happy enough. I was convinced that the foundation of what could be a good friendship was being laid.

We had eleven people at the One Voice meeting, as Britta had brought along a couple of her third-year roommates, who happened to be straight allies. We outlined next Saturday's Student Involvement Day event, finalized who would monitor the table and what games we might play in the grass, and confirmed who was bringing what for food.

"Remember, if we have the best cookies out of all the other clubs, we *will* attract attention," Britta reminded us. "So me and the girls here will make our famous megahuge chocolate chip snickerdoodles, because we have a kitchen in our apartment. Those cookies alone will gather a crowd."

I was appreciating Britta's positive spirit more and more with each meeting. She pushed her fingers through her white hair as she bragged about her cookie-making skill.

"I'm the only one who can do these cookies justice. I'll make them just before my turn at the table, and they'll be warm. The smell will grab students by the nose and haul them in."

From their spots beside each other to my left, Casey and Nate smiled.

I hope like hell Nate can find a place for Cindy to stay next weekend. I really want him to be at this rally with us. He can carry our table out to the quad and stand there like an LGBT bouncer.

Okay, gotta head. Casey's waiting for me. He's dragging me off to the library. Again. Midterms soon.

Call me, dude.

11
NATE'S DIARY

September 27

I WAKE up alone. I eat alone. I work alone. I come home alone. I sleep alone.

Sometimes I sit in my truck and listen to this song, "Here Without You" by 3 Doors Down, over and over again 'til my eyes are all friggin' misty.

Yeah. Wah, wah, wah. Poor fuckin' Nate.

Shit, I really ain't all alone. I got Cindy to take care of. And there's a few guys at work I shoot the shit with every now and then. And Missy behind the counter at the minimart. But it's not the same. Not like bein' with them two.

Almost wish I hadn't made love to 'em this past weekend.

Sounds fucked up, I know. But before, when they were away from me, I missed the hell outta 'em cuz I loved 'em so fuckin' much. But now I been *inside* 'em. Shit. This is gonna sound so friggin' messed up, but now I feel like I'm *mated* with Casey and Zander, like in those dumb vampire movies that Casey can't get enough of. Like I need to be near 'em—to look after 'em and stay on the same wavelength with 'em and keep on lovin' 'em with my body so they know who they belong to. Not just cuz of horniness neither.

So last night I woke up around two cuz I had a fucked-up nightmare. Those Queen Bees from high school were at Boston City College, and they were beatin' the livin' shit outta Casey—kinda like the way Uncle Rich beat the livin' shit outta me and how Liz Trainer kicked Casey's ass junior year of high school, but both put together. And I was watchin' it from far away. I couldn't get to him to help. Zander was callin' for me—screamin' for me, really—cuz all of these preppy college dudes were holdin' him back. They were physically holdin' on to him, cuz they wanted him to hang with them, I figure, and he couldn't get to Casey. And I was friggin' desperate, flailin' around in my bed, which is what woke me up.

And if I thought the dream was fucked up, it wasn't nothin' compared to the feelin's goin' on in my brain when I was lyin' there in bed, after the dream. I felt like I was all alone on a faraway planet, freezin' cold but sweatin' my ass off. Go figure. I was so damned sure I was gonna barf, I got outta bed and grabbed my trash can so I could hang on to it just in case.

Had to ask myself what the fuck was goin' on with me. I didn't miss the fact that just two years before, I was alone and I was cool with it. Cuz my natural way is to be a loner. Now I was practically cryin' cuz I missed two guys so fuckin' much.

When I woke up at two and couldn't get back to sleep for all the tryin' I did, there wasn't nothin' else for me to do than think. And question shit.

Are Casey and Zander actually gonna wait for me for four friggin' years?

Am I gonna end up alone and with a broken heart, worse even than when Mom got hauled off to jail?

Next thing I did was think about the topic Casey and Zander had made me promise I'd think on.

Is Uncle Rich gonna beat the livin' crap outta me every other week from now 'til Cindy's high school graduation?

Is there gonna be anything left of me to be with Casey and Zander?

More important than that, even—*is Cindy safe livin' here? Can I really protect her from Uncle Rich? And is Zander right? Is something freaky goin' on in Cindy's head that makes her need to see a shrink so she grows up to be some sort of normal?*

I thought about our situation with Uncle Rich for a long while. First off, I knew there was no talkin' it all out with Rich. He's not the listenin' sort of dude. He's rash and gets pissed off real easy. Comin' to any sort of an agreement with him is just not gonna happen.

For now at least, I can protect her just fine as long as I'm home when them two is home together, and I never let them two be alone without me for more than five minutes. If Cindy has to be here alone for a little while when I'm at work, she'll have to stay in her room and keep her trap shut. I'm gonna make her promise it as soon as she wakes up in the morning.

But outta respect for Casey and Zander, I'm decidin' on one more thing. I'll look around and see if there's another place for Cindy to live. A home where she'll be welcome and safe and where I'll be able to see her whenever I want.

Shit. It's nearly morning already, and Uncle Rich is screamin' bloody murder in the kitchen. Better go downstairs and see what's got him so pissed off.

CASEY'S REAL LIFE

I WAS at the library, yet again. But there's an excellent reason for that—it's almost time for midterms, and I have my work cut out for me. I chose a heavy course load because I want to double major in bio and maybe statistics. I wanted to get the core requirements out of the way as soon as possible so I'd have time to take a few classes for enjoyment senior year.

I knew I needed to study a lot, except during the Student Involvement Day event in the quad on Saturday. So I was okay with the fact that Nate couldn't come down this weekend, but at the same time, I also knew Zander was bitterly disappointed about it. He really wanted both of us there for One Voice's first big day as a club at BCC. But he controlled his disappointment valiantly when we spoke to Nate on the phone.

I had to study until my brain swelled up, so I probably wouldn't have been too much fun for Nate to hang out with anyway.

But I wasn't happy or relaxed about Nate's claim that he couldn't come down because he couldn't find a place for Cindy to stay. I had a strong feeling, like an instinct, that things weren't right with Nate. I hoped Rich hadn't beaten him up again.

I closed my notebook and placed my computer in my messenger bag. The library had a coffee shop on the bottom floor, and since I'd already been at the library for two hours, I thought I'd earned an iced latte. And I was going to call Nate. I wanted to get in touch with him before Zander arrived at the library as I thought Nate might feel less ganged up on if only one of us were asking questions.

Once I had my coffee and was sitting on one of the comfortable couches in the lobby, I placed the call to Nate.

"Casey?"

"Yes, it's me, Nate. Hi."

"This ain't our regular time to talk."

"Maybe I just wanted to hear your voice, sweetheart." I tried not to feel insulted by the lack of a greeting.

There was a moment of silence. "Uh… yeah. It's sure good to hear from ya, babe." His mouth sounded like it was stuffed full of cotton balls.

Not only that, but his tone of voice was controlled, even guarded. "Well, I'm just checking in. I wondered if you'd given what we talked about last Friday night any thought."

"Sure have. Thought on it in bed a couple of nights back."

"And?"

"And what?"

I sighed, thinking how similar discussing this topic with Nate was to pulling teeth. "Did you come to any conclusions?"

Predictably, there was another extended silence.

"Nate, sweetie, talk to me… please." I was essentially begging, but I didn't care. "You and Cindy aren't safe living with Rich. You know it, and I know it, and Zander knows it."

"I'm on speaker, ain't I? Zander's listening in… gonna pounce on me any second. And I ain't in the mood for that shit."

I fought the tears that instantly sprung into my eyes at his bitter tone. "No, Zander isn't listening in. I'm in the library, alone."

"Shit. Sorry, man."

This time I was the quiet one.

"Look, Casey. I thought on it. I'm keepin' my eyes open for another place where Cindy can live, that I know is safe for her and where she'd be happy at."

"What about your Aunt Terri's house?"

I knew he was nodding and I could picture his long hair bouncing up and down on his shoulders. "That's a real possibility. But I'm gonna have Cindy spend a few more weekends there. Make sure she likes it and that Aunt Terri gets to know her and like her... y'know, before I bring it up."

I smiled. This was the furthest we'd ever gotten in one of these conversations. "That's great, Nate. Thank you for taking our concerns so seriously. Now tell me why you sound like you're talking with a wad of cotton in your mouth." It wasn't *that* early. Nate should sound more awake. He'd have to be at work in forty-five minutes.

The ensuing silence told me everything. More than I wanted to know but certainly what I *needed* to know. And pretty much exactly what I'd suspected.

"He beat you up again, didn't he?"

More silence, which basically added up to a "Yeah."

"How bad is it this time?"

Nate's voice emerged from the silence, deep and rumbly. "Not too bad, babe."

My battle against tears was lost. "Tell... tell me."

"Ain't nothin', 'kay?" He cleared his throat. "It's like this. He came home late a couple nights ago, pissed off that I parked in his spot."

"Nate...."

"I'd been sleepin' mostly, and thinkin' some, when I heard him screamin'. Went downstairs to check it out and—."

"He hit you in the mouth?"

"A few times. Got a loose-ish tooth. On the side. Little bit of swellin'. No biggie."

I swallowed hard. "This is *not* okay, Nate. What's happening to you is not okay."

"I know it... but don't tell Zander, 'kay? He don't need to worry, and he gets so riled up it's hard for me to deal with and shit. I got this—no worries."

I sobbed. Thankfully it was still pretty early, and the library lobby wasn't too crowded. "You don't 'got this.' I'm telling Zander. There are three of us in this, and there will be no secrets." I took a deep breath in an effort to calm myself. "You know that."

"Whatever." He exhaled heavily.

"Do you need to see a dentist, Nate?" He had no dental insurance, so I was ready to offer whatever help he needed.

"Nah. Tooth seems to be tightening back up."

Well, that little piece of news nearly killed me. "Just come here this weekend and bring Cindy."

I heard a loud exhale of breath. "No can do, dude. Cindy got her first high school dance on Saturday night. Told her I'd drive her. Can't let her down."

It was my turn to breathe out noisily. "Then next weekend— definitely. It's a three-day weekend, and we want you with us. So start looking now for a place for Cindy to stay."

"Done. Your wish is my command."

"Right." It came out sounding sarcastic, but I didn't care.

"It'll be okay, Casey. I got this."

I stood up, knowing a trip to the men's room was in order before I got back to studying. I had to wash the tears off my face, at a minimum. "I love you, Nate. Stay away from Rich, please."

"I promise I'll keep clear of him, best I can."

"We'll Skype you tonight, right after dinner."

"If you're gonna Skype me, maybe you better prepare Zander for what you guys're gonna see. My mouth, y'know."

I gasped. It was against my will, as I was doing my best to play it cool, but the sound escaped nonetheless. "Nate...."

"No worries, babe. I got this."

It was as if by repeating "I got this" Nate could convince himself, and me, that he actually had the situation under control—which he clearly didn't.

ZANDER ZANE'S One Voice Blog Spot—by invite only

Your host, Zander Z

***Part I. Personal shit – not for public*

Hey, Dan.

For a little while at least, I think I'm gonna divide my posts. I can't focus on my public One Voice blog if I haven't gotten my personal shit off my chest. So since you're my only loyal follower at this point, I'll devote the start of each post to what's going on personally and then shift into One-Voice-business mode.

But before I unload my problems, I want to say thank you. Thanks for calling the other night. Thanks for assuring me that you'll always love who I love. Knowing that you love Casey and Nate—that the fact that there are *two people* who mean the world to me isn't something you'd even blink at—was exactly what I needed to hear from my big bro. *Exactly.*

You're really more than a brother to me. Let's face it—you helped raise me. I look up to you and want to make you proud. Knowing that my choices are cool in your eyes is vital. Okay—end of mushiness now. But thank you.

Things with Nate are just as complicated as usual. He's been getting the shit beat outta him by his uncle on a fairly regular basis, and he won't do anything to stop it. He just takes it. Nate's philosophy seems to be that as long as Uncle Rich isn't messing with Cindy, then everything's cool. But he's so wrong. Casey and I know this. He may even know it, deep down. He says he's trying to figure out another place where she can live while she finishes high school, but he doesn't seem to be in any kind of rush.

Someday soon, D-man, the shit is gonna hit the fan at the DeMarco house. And I'm fucking worried about it. My biggest fear is that Rich will—fuck, it's hard to write this—maybe even *kill* Nate. He'll maybe get carried away in a beating and not stop until it's too late. I've seen Rich in action. And even though Nate could kick his ass, he just doesn't fight back.

I love the dude. Casey loves the dude. We need him to be here in Boston with us where we know he's safe. It's hard as hell to concentrate on my classes and my goals for One Voice when I'm consumed with worry about Nate's safety.

Our goal is to get him to stay here for the long Columbus Day weekend. Show him how awesome it would be if he lived with us. The second he agrees to moving to Boston, Casey and I have agreed we're gonna try to move out of our dorm and into a one-bedroom apartment with Nate.

***PART II.* One Voice business.

The day after tomorrow is Student Involvement Day, where all of the school's clubs line up along the paved walkway in the quad and try to recruit new members. One Voice will be there. Our table is located right between the BCC Acoustics Club and Recreational Cooking at the City College (RCACC). With at least three volunteers staffing the table all day, gourmet cookies and whoopie pies, Lady Gaga music, and rainbow flags, my hope is that we get ten more members by the end of the day. So wish us luck.

12
NATE'S DIARY

October 1

RIGHT NOW, pretty much exactly, Casey and Zander are at Student Involvement Day, sittin' at a rainbow-covered table in the quad with the One Voice sign stuck in the grass in front of it. It's nighttime now, so they're probably wearin' their BCC sweatshirts, snugglin' together to stay warm, eatin' Britta's chocolate chip snickerdoodle cookies, probably all tired out from playin' on the lawn with the rainbow Frisbee and gettin' down to Lady Gaga tunes.

And I'm here at home, guardin' Cindy from my asshole Uncle Rich.

Nursin' a brand new fat lip I just got courtesy of the asshole before I dropped Cindy off at her dance, cuz he said, since she didn't do the fuckin' dishes, she shouldn't be allowed to go. Course, I stood up to him, told him the girl was goin' to her goddammed dance, and he laid me out flat on the kitchen floor. Took her to the friggin' dance anyhow.

This *so* sucks.

Just miss them two so bad.

Wish like hell I was down at BCC, helpin' to recruit new volunteers for the One Voice Club. It's the right thing to do, and it'd make Zander real happy.

This sucks.

I know one thing. I ain't goin' back home 'til after the damn dance. Not too excited to meet up with Uncle Rich and his overactive fists. Maybe I'll just go over to the minimart and shoot the shit with Missy 'til I gotta go pick up Cindy at Benjamin Franklin High School.

ZANDER ZANE'S One Voice Blog Spot—by invite only

Your host, Zander Z

Got ten new people, maybe even twelve, at the Student Involvement Day rally. Most of them were dudes, but we got maybe three more girls too. So I'm super pumped. And we had a decent-size crowd at the table for most of the day and right into the night.

Britta's stellar cookies didn't hurt our cause. Some kids took One Voice's club information home with them and said they were gonna think about whether or not to join, so we may even get more members over the next few weeks.

I stuck around the One Voice table all day and right up until nine at night when we shut it down. I only took a quick break to take a piss in the Porta Pottis down by the library, right after lunch. Casey stayed for most of the day too. But in the early afternoon, he said he had to go and hit the books. Everybody who'd signed up to contribute in the club meetings came at the right time and brought what they'd promised. So it was all good.

And only one thing was missing. Nate DeMarco.

I can't think too hard about that right now. The subject gets me down, and I still gotta write up a positive article for the school newspaper saying what an extraordinary success One Voice's participation in Student Involvement Day was for our club.

But this whole situation that Casey, Nate, and I are caught in just isn't fair. In fact, it really bites. But it's Wednesday, and if everything goes according to plan, our partner will be here in two nights. Hope like hell everything goes according to plan.

I know I may seem like the strong one, the level-headed one, but I need them—*both* of them.

13

NATE'S DIARY

COLUMBUS DAY WEEKEND
October 7

I'M SO fuckin' psyched. Cindy's got a friend who said she could come and stay Friday after school 'til friggin' Monday, seein' as it's a long holiday weekend and all. So right after work, I'm gonna make sure Cindy's packed, take her to Mickey D's for a burger, and then bring her over to her friend, Madison's, house. And I'm gonna fill her pockets with cash. There's this fair up north in NH that Madison's dad is gonna take 'em to. I want her to have an awesome time. Cuz I know I'll be havin' a fuckin' awesome time with my guys.

I been doin' a lot of thinkin' cuz I promised my guys I would. And I came to the conclusion that maybe I oughtta talk to my Aunt Terri sooner rather than later, and see if she can take Cindy in for the rest of her time in high school. Cindy seems to be okay with Aunt Terri, and she likes Jana good enough. Plus, I'd be only fifteen minutes away from her if I lived near Boston City College with Casey and Zander.

I ain't plannin' on mentionin' nothin' to Cindy 'til I check it out with Aunt Terri. Then I'll have to prepare myself for the predictable explosion. Not sure if Cindy's gonna be too thrilled with uprootin' herself from her school and friends and shit. So far, I been the only one who's got beaten on. Probably she thinks it ain't never gonna happen to her. But I'm pretty damn sure it's gonna eventually be her turn for a beatin' if we stick around here with Uncle Rich, and cuz of that I think I'll be able to get her to see reason if I try hard enough.

Gonna tell Casey and Zander all about my plan this weekend. Them two are gonna be totally psyched.

I get to spend a weekend in seventh fuckin' heaven, and I can't wait 'til tomorrow.

CASEY'S REAL LIFE

WHEN NATE arrived Friday night, I didn't hold back. I basically attacked the man.

After I finally released him from my grasp—yes, I eventually had to let go of him with both my arms *and* my legs—he was grinning, and his eyes were sparkling with what might have been happy tears.

"I missed you," I said when I stepped back to look at him, but I couldn't stop myself from scanning his face, looking for evidence of new and old bruises. And unfortunately he wore evidence of both, a puffy lip and scattered yellowing marks.

Nate bent down and kissed me thoroughly. "I missed ya too, babe."

Zander, as usual, waited patiently through our long kiss. Or *two kisses*, since I very well may have grasped Nate around the neck and pulled him down for one more smooch. And then I tugged on Nate's hand, drew him to the grass near the parking lot where Zander stood, and pushed them together. "Hug and kiss, you guys."

I loved watching them greet each other. I knew they missed each other as much as I missed Nate, but they were more reserved than I was. For a couple of seconds, they just stood and stared at each other. I would call it "drinking each other in with their eyes," but I wouldn't say that out loud because they would both roll their eyes and say it was too dramatic, even if it was true. Nate placed his hands on Zander's hips and pulled him in so their chests were pressed together. Zander, who tried so hard to be our emotional rock, let himself be pulled in and rested his head on Nate's shoulder.

I observed quietly as Nate patted the middle of Zander's back. And Zander just slumped against Nate and let Nate love him.

"Kiss. Go ahead, kiss each other," I suggested breathlessly.

Very obediently, Nate tilted Zander's face with his hand and softly touched his lips to Zander's. When the kiss was over, Zander reached up to Nate's swollen bottom lip and touched it with his thumb. I started to worry that Zander was going to say something about it and I knew the time was not yet right.

"Come on." Suddenly I was impatient. "Let's go back to our room."

I wanted to be alone with them so badly that I started to run in the direction of the dormitory. Once they got Nate's bag out of the truck, my boyfriends trotted behind me.

"I WANT you both so much." There my voice went, again speaking without my permission. "Please take your clothes off now."

Nate and Zander looked at each other and smiled. Then Nate winked at Zander. "What do ya say we get *our boy* into his birthday suit first, huh?"

And that was how all the fun got started. The two of them removed my clothes, piece by piece, until I stood before them naked—and shivering a little because we'd left the window open a crack to make the room feel fresh. "I put the fancy sheets back on the bed. Right after me and Zander pushed the beds together this afternoon."

Nate winked, but it was directed at me this time. "Well, I guess it's time we got you inside of there."

He pulled back the sheets, and I slid to the very center of the bed, as I knew they expected. I watched as Nate and Zander pulled off their T-shirts. When their chests were bare, I couldn't help but admire the masculinity of their forms.

Nate was bigger than Zander, more broad, muscle-bound, and bulky. He also had a fair amount of dark hair on his chest, which masked the healing bruises pretty well. And Zander's smooth chest, his whole body really, was well-defined and toned—the body of a runner or a soccer player. They both sported some leftover color from their summer tans, and I think I was drooling before they even started unbuttoning their jeans.

I noticed that they didn't watch each other the way I was watching them as they disrobed. They always acted more detached with one another. But I could still see them taking sneaky glances when they thought nobody was looking. It didn't bother me that they behaved this way. *Reserved* was how they were with each other. I thought this selective shyness was about as sweet as could be.

Once they were naked, they slipped in on either side of me. I pointed out, "Zander, you didn't get to make love to Nate when we were together the weekend before last."

Zander gasped predictably, and Nate turned bright red, also predictably. "I made love to him," he said defensively.

"You know what I mean, Zander." The look on his face told me he knew precisely what I was talking about. And Nate knew too. Magenta blushes don't lie. "You didn't go *inside* his body."

They both nodded and looked at me, as if for direction.

"I think that should be where we start."

Again my boyfriends nodded.

"Well, good. I like it when we're in agreement." I reached my arms up and pulled them both in for a three-way kiss.

I could tell by the way they kissed, their lips tight and controlled, that Nate and Zander were nervous—much more so than they had been when we first made love a few weeks before. I set my mind to getting them in the best possible position to move past their anxiety. So I decided I was going to do something I'd been wanting to do for quite some time.

First I got up on my knees and backed out from my spot between them. "Lie right beside each other on your backs. And Nate, pull Zander toward you so his head is on your chest."

My lovers looked up at me with wide eyes but didn't move.

"Go ahead, you guys. Get moving." I smiled at their blank expressions. Once they dutifully arranged themselves this way, though, I lifted Zander's leg and draped it over Nate's, locking them together. "This is how I want you guys to stay." Then I bent down and pushed my face into the area between Nate's legs and, a few seconds later, against Zander's privates, which were in pretty close proximity to each other. I breathed him in. Then I went back to Nate and took him in my mouth. I stroked Zander with my hand while I loved Nate with my tongue and lips. I really had no clue what I was doing, so I just went with what I thought would feel good on me. After a couple of minutes, I switched and took Zander in my mouth.

Oral sex was clearly a new experience for Zander. He gasped when I took him between my lips and continued to breathe heavily as I explored him. Nate, it seemed, had a sudden urge to swallow each of Zander's gasps. When I looked up at them, Nate had tilted Zander's head up with his hand the way he had done in the parking lot and sealed his lips over Zander's. The sight was so perfect that I paused to watch.

"I wanna make love to you, Nate." Zander's voice was gruff when Nate finally released his lips. "Can I get inside you?"

Nate nodded and asked simply, "How do ya want me?"

"All fours, okay?"

I sat up as they got into position, and then I leaned over and got the lubricant off the bedside table. Nate, so big, burly, and sometimes even wary, appeared supremely vulnerable. It was not a way I was accustomed to perceiving him. Zander tapped my arm to break me from my daze. He held out his hand, and I squirted lubricant on his fingers. He rubbed his fingers against mine to share the lubricant, and then we got Nate ready.

Nate was completely silent as we touched him so intimately. His breathing was very controlled, and I thought his whole body seemed rigid. So when Zander was slowly entering him, I knelt beside Nate and massaged his body—the arm that was nearest to me, his shoulders, even his thigh.

"Kiss me, Casey. Please." It almost sounded like Nate was pleading with me—as if he needed an additional intimate connection with me while Zander made his way into his body.

So I lay flat, almost directly beneath Nate, and put my face where he could easily access it with his lips. Zander pressed time and again into Nate's body, while Nate's lips found mine and stayed there, unmoving. The inside of his bottom lip was swollen into a hard lump and cut on the right, and I knew that meant Rich had punched him very hard. Hard enough to make Nate bleed. I suddenly felt protective of him. I wanted to comfort him, to please him—to take him away from the pain of his life. I grabbed his penis with one hand and mine with the other. I stroked and stroked, keeping time to the sounds of Zander's pleasure above us.

"Wanna come all together… like all at the same time," Zander uttered from behind Nate. "And I'm getting close."

Nate also seemed close to orgasm, as was I. "Can you wait just a few more seconds, Zander?" I managed to ask.

Zander grunted, and Nate didn't utter a sound, as he was beyond speech—which was fine. Zander and I were in charge of his body, and I loved that he had given himself over to us completely.

And a few seconds later, I heard, "I'm gonna… g-gonna… now…." Zander did his best to warn us. "Come with m-me."

And so we did. All three of us, as one being, released the love in our hearts and gave it to each other.

NATE WAS almost bashful after we made love… or after he took such a submissive position in lovemaking. Like Zander and in many ways me, Nate hadn't been given many reasons to trust people. I understood that his ability to maintain a rough, scary image was the ace in his pocket. He relied on it when everything else failed him. It protected him and defended him. He hid behind it. Loving him as we had, and in particular, as Zander had, we had taken that away from him. We had made him soft, sweet, and vulnerable. He needed some time to adjust to this new Nate.

Luckily Zander also understood this and quickly made a plan for the night so Nate didn't have to feel so openly awkward. We spent the evening at Quincy Market and ate dinner at

Bangkok Express. Then we went to Boston Chipyard, where we indulged in the best cookies I ever tasted, with the exception of Britta's chocolate chip snickerdoodles. After that, the three of us headed to the Museum of Science, where we saw a laser show set to rock music.

By the time we got to the laser show, Nate was back to his usual self—still quiet and reserved but less awkward. I wanted to put him between us so both of us could cuddle with him. But he wanted me in the middle, which was the position with which the guys seemed most comfortable, especially in public. During the laser show, I held their hands on my lap, and I made sure to push their hands together without mine between them every now and then. The night out together was a real date. It was fun, delicious, loud, shiny, and everything we needed as a throuple.

WE TOOK Nate to breakfast at the student cafeteria, where we met up with Anna and Claire. Nate seemed to be more relaxed in their presence than last time, and I was also becoming more and more relaxed with them. They didn't seem like "regular" young women, or at all like the stereotype I had developed of them during my years at Benjamin Franklin High School. They were more like real people to me, like my mom, my sisters, and Nate's sister, Cindy, when she was on good behavior.

"Nate, I was thinking about you the other day when I saw this amazing mixed-breed puppy—lab and golden retriever, I think. A student was walking her in the quad." Claire seemed eager to talk to Nate.

"And let me tell you, Claire was all over that puppy as soon as the owner said it was okay to pat her. I couldn't separate her from little Beyoncé for maybe thirty minutes," Anna chimed in.

"Beyoncé? The student named the dog Beyoncé?" I had to laugh and wonder what the *real* Beyoncé would think of that.

"Yeah," Claire replied. "The dog's owner is a big fan."

We all ate our bacon, egg, and cheese bagel sandwiches, which were on special, and talked about puppies, movies, and favorite flavors of ice cream. Nothing heavy, and that was just perfect.

"So, how long are you staying? Monday's a holiday, but Tuesday is One Voice's big event—the National Coming Out Day rally in the quad. Is there any way you can stay for it?" Claire seemed to really like Nate.

But at her question, Nate's eyes got wide, and he immediately shook his head. "Uh... no. That ain't a possibility."

"Why not? Do you have to work?"

Nate had already informed Zander and me that he didn't have to work until Tuesday night, but still he nodded.

"Can't you call in sick?" Claire apparently had a persistent side.

So I stepped in to rescue him. "He can't miss a single day of work. They give him most weekends off, so they expect him to have excellent attendance on weekdays."

Claire nodded sympathetically, but none of us missed the way Zander hung his head in apparent disappointment. And I didn't miss that Nate stared at him, taking in Zander's crestfallen posture.

"There will be other events I'm sure you'll be able to attend," Anna offered by way of consolation.

Zander kept his eyes fixed on the floor, and Nate kept his eyes fixed on Zander.

"Um... these bagel sandwiches sure are good. How about if we go get you another one, Nate? You're so big—you must need two." Claire stood up and snagged Nate by the sleeve. "Come on." She dragged him toward the service counter, in an effort to snap him out of his unhappy trance.

I reached for Zander and squeezed his knee. I didn't need to say that Nate would stay here for the rally if he could. We both knew it.

He lifted his shoulders and said in a low tone, "Yeah, I know." Then he got up and headed to the men's room.

Anna looked squarely at me. "There's more going on here than Claire and I are aware of, hmm?"

"Yes, that's true," I admitted, wanting to share it with her but not sure if it would be okay with Nate.

"Well, if we can help in any way, at any time, just let us know." She leaned over and squeezed my knee in much the same way I had squeezed Zander's. It was the first time a girl this age had touched me since the beating I had taken at the hands of the high school bully, Liz Trainer. And I hadn't recoiled or made an excuse to follow Zander to the bathroom. In fact, my reaction had been quite the opposite. I covered her hand with mine.

"Thank you, Anna. You and Claire are quite wonderful friends."

And I meant it.

14
NATE'S DIARY

October 9

BROUGHT MY journal along this weekend. What the fuck is with that, eh? It's like I'm so used to writin' shit down when I'm tryin' to deal with it that I sort of *need* this notebook. Casey says that writin' is how I absorb the shit that's goin' down in my life. He calls it "processing my thoughts." Guess he's right.

Anyhow it's Sunday night and we just got done with eatin' some pretty stellar pizza we got delivered to their dorm room. And it ain't no rumor—college kids put down a lot of that shit. Now we're gonna head over to the One Voice meetin'. Worst part of that is I'm havin a friggin' ton of back and forth thoughts about leavin' on Monday and missin' Zander's big day on Tuesday. I know he gets why I gotta go home, but I also know he's disappointed as hell that I ain't gonna be there. Shit. Nobody never wanted me to be at their special day in my whole entire life, and here's this dude who won't enjoy his big moment as much if yours truly ain't there. And I'm skippin' out on him.

Before the pizza came, I texted Cindy to see if she could stay one more night at her friend's house. That was a big no-can-do. Her friend's mom was like, "That girl's leavin' Monday afternoon cuz we gotta go food shoppin' and pick up Grandpa at the airport and blah, blah, blah." Me and Cindy got the picture nice and clear. So it looks like I'm gonna have to split on Monday by lunchtime, which was gonna just about kill me to do. So much that I'm sittin' in my car, scribblin' in my notebook about how fuckin' ruined I am when I think of ditchin' Zander on his big day.

I fuckin' love these guys so much it nearly hurts. Never felt half this much for nobody in my life, 'cept for maybe Cindy. I'm in heaven when I'm here with 'em. Fit in here like nowhere else. It's gettin' harder and harder to leave each week after I see 'em. Add to that, disappointin' my boy, Zander. I gotta figure somethin' out. Gotta find a way to stay.

Don't think nothin' is worth hurtin' Zander for.

zanderZ@catchme.com

Bro—

I need your help. Or maybe I just want you to listen to me. Whatever the case, I've gotta get in touch with you because the shit totally hit the fan yesterday. It's fucked-up, and *it's my fault*. Dan, I got Nate to stay overnight on Monday. He knew he shouldn't have, but I made him feel guilty for abandoning me when I "needed him" most.

So, shit. He stayed. Nate stayed *for me*. And on Tuesday afternoon, he gets this call from his aunt. She said Nate's little sister is in some hospital in Central NH and Nate had better get his ass home. Nate's uncle finally did it, man. He beat the shit out of Cindy, Nate's fourteen-year-old sister.

One fucking night. For one fucking night, Nate left them alone. And that dude couldn't keep his paws off her. All Nate could tell us was what his aunt told him—that Cindy said Rich tried to choke her to death.

Need you now, man. So bad.

No more One Voice Blog, in case you're wondering. Priorities.

Z

zanderZ@catchme.com

Danny—

Thanks for trying to call me. Sorry I missed it. Shit is just crazy around here. I tried to get you back a few minutes ago, but you must be in your evening class now. Listen, dude, we can't reach Nate. He took off from here today at like 3:30 p.m., after the call from his aunt, saying, "Gotta head out." He was acting like somebody lit a fire under his ass. Now it's seven, and he hasn't answered our calls or texts. I know he's at the hospital and is occupied with other shit, but he must know we're trying to reach him.

Casey is *losing it*. As in, completely. First of all, I know the whole idea of somebody being beat up so badly that they have to be hospitalized brings back memories of the assault on him during junior year, because that's pretty much exactly what happened to him. Second, I think he feels partly responsible for what happened to Cindy because he never told his parents about the violence that was going on in Nate and Cindy's home. But Nate had begged him not to. He always told us "I got this." And we knew he didn't "got" nothing, but we never called him on it, even though we saw his black eyes and the swollen lips and all the bruises. And third, Casey is freaking panicking because Nate won't answer the phone or texts. Shit, we even tried to e-mail him but haven't heard a word.

We wanna be beside Nate in the hospital, but it'd be fucked up just to show up there without talking to him. Not even sure which hospital, at this point.

We don't have his aunt's number either.

This situation is so fucking screwed up.

Need help.

Z

zanderZ@catchme.com

Dan—

Thanks for calling. Hearing your voice was super essential. And for the record, I don't give a crap that you called after midnight. It's not like Casey and I were sleeping or anything. We're still waiting for a call from Nate.

A call that I'm beginning to doubt is gonna come. At least any time soon.

This shit is so royally fucked up.

I keep questioning myself and my role in this whole pile of stinking crap. Nate was gonna leave Monday afternoon, and I started acting all sulky and silent. On purpose, dude. Like a spoiled fucking brat. I was trying to let him know that I wasn't happy about him taking off on me at One Voice's biggest moment so far at BCC.

It's because of all the shit that went down with Casey in high school that my eyes were opened. I just got committed to the fact that people ought to be able to be who they are—to love who they love—without fear of harsh judgment or physical violence. Coming Out Day meant something major to me. It *means* something to me still. But guilt-tripping Nate into sticking around may be something that none of us can ever forgive me for.

To make me happy, Nate said he'd stay. He called Cindy, and I could hear him tell her to steer clear of Uncle Rich. He said that after school she should just go to her bedroom and stay there 'til he got home from Boston, which would be just after dinnertime, and that he'd check on her and feed her before he went to work. And then he hung up and tried to put on a happy face for me and Casey, but I could tell he was worried as all hell.

On Monday night, the three of us managed to push all bad thoughts aside. We made love for pretty much half the night. After he made love to me the last time, Nate held me for like an hour. Casey had dropped off to sleep before we'd had a chance to put him between us like we always did.

As he was holding me, he said, "Sorry, man. Sorry that I was *gonna* leave ya. Didn't wanna miss Coming Out Day and bein' there for ya, but sometimes I feel like I am gettin' pulled in all different directions."

And like a fucking clueless douchebag, I said, "You're forgiven. No harm done." Or something along those lines. Then we kind of rolled Casey in between us, snuggled up to him, and drifted off to sleep with fucking satisfied grins on our lips.

I feel like a total piece of shit. Lowly as hell.

Dude, I put my precious One Voice rally before the very safety of Nate's sister.

Don't know if Nate will ever forgive me for that.

Don't know if Casey will forgive me either.

Fuck, man, I don't know if I'll ever forgive myself for what I've done.

Later—

Z

15
CASEY'S REAL LIFE

FINALLY I called my parents last night and told them about it. All of it. I told them about the abuse that has been going on at Nate's house and that I'd known about it ever since I met him. I told them how Nate had assured us he had everything under control, and I'd just let myself believe him because the alternative was unknown, and because of that, too difficult.

My parents were definitely disappointed in me. I think it's going to take a while for them to understand why I kept my mouth shut about Nate and Cindy's suffering. For that matter, it's going to take some time for *me* to figure out why I never stepped forward and said, "No more, Nate. This is wrong."

Mom and Dad told me they would try to confirm which hospital Cindy is in. They also said they would check on Nate and find out if his uncle had been arrested, as it was a matter of public record. I told them I wanted to come home from school and look for Nate myself, but they said there was nothing I could do. If Nate was ready to see us, he would have called us back. He clearly hadn't sufficiently worked through his pain and guilt. I knew they were right.

Ultimately if Nate wanted to talk to us, he knew our number. He knew he could call any hour of the day or night and we'd jump to help him. He just didn't want to talk to us.

Nate did not want contact with Zander and me.

Which was a bitter pill to swallow.

Lying in my twin bed, I turned my head and gazed across the room at Zander. He was stretched out, covered in blankets, flat on his back in his tiny twin bed. I could tell he wasn't sleeping, just from the way his chest lifted and fell. And his staggered breathing told me he was agitated too. But I couldn't reach out to him. The pain was too fresh. The uncertainty was too looming.

For the first time in years, I dreaded the next day.

zanderZ@catchme.com

Dan—

Just read an article in the newspaper that said New Hampshire resident Richard J. DeMarco has been arrested for second degree assault and has not been released on bail. They didn't mention Cindy's name, probably because she's a minor. So I don't know much, but at least I know the asshole's in jail, where he belongs.

It's been three days, and still no word from Nate. Me and Casey haven't given up on calling and texting him. We've been leaving him long messages about how much we love him.

Mr. and Mrs. Minton tried to find out how Cindy's doing, but they haven't had much luck with the local hospitals. It's all confidential info, and the hospitals mean business when they say that. At least Casey and I know Nate is *alive*, because Mr. Minton stopped by Nate's house, and he was getting into his truck to go to work. Casey's dad told us that he hopped out of the car and went to the truck to talk to Nate. Nate wouldn't allow himself to be drawn into conversation. He wouldn't even look Mr. Minton in the eyes.

Mr. Minton shouted at the truck as it backed out of the driveway, "The boys are concerned, and they want to talk to you!" Either Nate didn't hear, or he pretended he didn't hear.

Mrs. Minton is gonna stop by the gas station tomorrow to see if she can get him to talk.

I'm relieved to know Nate's okay, but I'm crushed to know that he has no interest in talking to us. And Casey is acting really weird with me. It reminds me of that very distant way he acted in high school after those bitchy girls screwed with him. He's here with me, but he isn't really present. He's being polite to me, but he's not being *himself*. I'd bet my life that he blames this whole thing on me. If I'd let Nate leave on Monday like he was supposed to, none of this would have happened.

Gotta study. Hope I can keep my mind on ethics. At least I'll see Anna and Claire in class. I'm not usually one to tell the world about my problems, but I've confided in these girls, and I'm glad I did. They're helping to keep me sane.

I'm out.

Zander

CASEY'S REAL LIFE

ON SUNDAY night, when Zander and I left the One Voice meeting and walked back toward our dorm, I finally let myself cry. That's the understatement of the century. Nate would have said I freaked out in a major way, but Nate wasn't around. Good thing Zander was ready for it, so he reacted to my tears and my ranting and raving with something close to grace.

As we made our way through the chilly courtyard, Zander reached for my hand. To warm me, to connect us, to let me know he was there for me—it didn't much matter why. I was mad and I was hurting and I was not going to let Zander think that I didn't blame him for blowing everything in this relationship sky high.

I snatched my hand out of his. "Don't touch me." I was actually shocked at the caustic sound of my voice. I couldn't remember ever behaving that way before—ever *feeling* that way before.

"Wha-what?" Zander was also shaken by my vehemence.

"I don't want you to touch me." I didn't think. I just spoke.

Zander stopped. "Why? Why, Casey?"

I shook my head. "Without him, I'm not complete. *We're* not complete." My eyes filled, and I didn't bother trying to control my tears. I couldn't stop them if I wanted to. "It hurts too much and...."

His hands dropped to his sides, but his fingers twitched, as if with an unmet need to touch me. His mouth fell open, but he didn't speak.

"Why did you have to send him on such a major guilt trip about going back home and missing your precious One Voice rally? You know he has a responsibility to Cindy!"

Zander didn't reply.

"We just needed to be patient with him while he worked out where Cindy could live. You just couldn't wait, could you?"

Now his eyes were wet, and I'd never seen him look so dejected. "No... I guess I couldn't wait."

I was hurt and angry, and now I was starting to feel guilty for blaming Zander for a situation that he truly did not create.

"It's all my fault, Casey... and maybe if you go to see Nate without me, he'll take you back. I'm the one who messed this thing up."

A few more agonizing seconds passed before I accepted that it was the situation I was upset with, not Zander. "Listen, Zander, I'm sorry." My regret, though not immediate, was intense. "I know it's not your fault." He needed to know my feelings of aversion to his touch were truly not just because I blamed him. My emotions were far more complicated than that. "It's just, Zander, since I healed, you know, *emotionally*, from what happened to me junior year, you've *both* been part of my life. Part of me. I just don't know how to *do this* without him."

"*Do this*?" He looked so confused.

"I don't know how to be a complete person without both of you." That was the only way to explain it. I wiped the tears off my cheeks, but more soon replaced them.

Thankfully, Zander nodded. "I get it."

"I am afraid to lean on you. On *just* you, that is... but I'm not angry at you. I'm more angry with *me*, in truth."

"Why are you angry with yourself?"

"I didn't stand up and say 'It's time for this to end' when it came to the abuse. I knew...." I was starting to sob a bit. "I knew that it was gonna end with something bad, and I didn't do the right thing because I thought we might... I thought we might *lose him.*"

Zander stepped forward and wrapped his arms around my shoulders. I needed those arms and his strength as well. I didn't fight his touch. I just cried.

"Casey, maybe this isn't anybody's fault but Rich DeMarco's."

"But I should've said something and—"

"You weren't responsible, Casey. If anyone is, it's me." He squeezed me harder.

"No, you're not, Zander. *No.*" I lifted my arms to hold on to his shoulders. "We need to stick together. Don't we. *Don't we?*"

Zander let out a sob and whispered in my ear, through his own tears, "Yeah, Casey. We need to stick together so that we can get through to Nate."

"So we can be a... a throuple... again."

Zander made an effort to smile at me, and I appreciated it. I needed to see a smile from someone I loved.

We stood in the brisk October night, hanging on to each other tightly until our fingers and noses and toes were frozen.

zanderZ@catchme.com

Hey, Dan.

It's been a freaking week since we talked to Nate. A week. And no, I'm not blaming myself for the shit hitting the fan like I did last week. At first, Casey blamed me too, but we've talked and agreed that mostly Nate's uncle was to blame. I appreciate you reminding me, in your last e-mail, that *I* didn't do this to Cindy. It really helped, and I really needed to hear it. But like I said, I also know I'm not totally free of blame. Casey and I shouldn't have just stood by and watched for almost two years while Nate got the shit kicked outta him on a regular basis. And we should have done something about Rich's constant threats toward Cindy.

So we have a plan, dude. If we don't talk to Nate this week, we're gonna go home for the weekend and barge in on him at his house. Think that's a good idea? I remember back when Casey refused to see us junior year after he was assaulted, and we barged in on him with his mother's permission. It worked—we got through to him. So maybe it'll work with Nate too.

Sounds like things are going great with you and Abby, though. You two are so solid. I can't help but be a bit jealous about that, but not jealous in a negative sense. Just jealous in a wish-it-was-us way.

I've got my hopes up that you'll bring Abby home for Thanksgiving this year. I know it's not an awesome celebration here or anything—there's just Ma, sometimes a stray aunt or cousin, and Ma's latest squeeze—but you've been to Abby's house for the past two Turkey Days, dude. This year I could sure use some brotherly love and sort-of-sisterly advice.

I'm going frigging crazy with worry and missing him.

I'm out.

Z

16

CASEY'S REAL LIFE

IF NATE had any interest in saying anything to me, he would say I was "freakin' out to the max" as we drove to his house on Friday night. He clearly didn't want to see or speak to us, but we were tracking him down, in the hope that he just needed a little push to open up.

Zander was driving Mom's Volvo. I was, it seemed, the perpetual passenger in life. I never had a strong urge to get behind the wheel, although I did have my license. But that night I couldn't have driven if I'd wanted to. I was literally trembling in fear of this pending confrontation.

"Nobody's home." We pulled into the dirt driveway and saw that Nate's truck wasn't there.

"Let's just knock on the door, Zander. Maybe his truck is being serviced." We both knew Nate serviced his own truck, but to humor me, Zander parked and got out. I did the same.

"Careful on the steps, dude." Zander was always looking out for me. He locked his hand on my elbow to support me.

"These stairs need to be fixed. They're totally hazardous." I wasn't sure why I said that. I just needed to say something.

Once I got to the top of the crumbling steps, I knocked a few times. Zander leaned past me, pressed his hands against the window beside the door, and looked inside the house. No one answered, which was what I expected, but Zander didn't step back. "Hey, Casey, check it out inside." He pushed me in front of him. "In the corner."

"Are those signs? Like maybe real estate signs?" No sooner had the words left my lips than my mind started scrambling for answers. "Why are there real estate signs—house-for-rent signs—in there, Zander?"

"And look. None of their junk is in there. See? None of Nate's games are on the shelf. And none of Cindy's magazines. And not even any ashtrays or beer cans everywhere like usual."

I nodded. The place was cleaner than I'd ever seen it and very bare. "What do you think?"

Zander placed his hand on my elbow again. "I think…." He stopped speaking and took a deep breath, then escorted me down the stairs. "I don't think Nate's living here anymore."

The earth seemed to move beneath my feet. "What are you talking about?"

We both turned to stare at the apparently unoccupied house. "Casey, it's after his work hours. His truck isn't here. His stuff isn't here. The place is clean. There are for-rent signs leaning in the corner of the living room. Add it up." He wasn't being sarcastic. He was just forcing me to look at the facts.

"I want to go home." I suddenly had an overwhelming desire to pull the covers over my head in my rainbow-colored childhood bedroom. "Take me home."

AFTER BREAKFAST the next morning, Mom, Dad, Zander, and I sat around the kitchen table sipping cups of herbal tea as the girls played Uno on the floor beside us. I knew my parents worried that I would fall into another depression. When I came home the night before and went straight to my room without a word to anyone, they were probably extremely concerned. But Zander slept beside me in my bed and held me as I tossed and turned. He woke me in the morning, despite my pleas to leave me be so I could sleep all day. That morning, sitting with my parents and one of my boyfriends, I knew I had done the right thing by getting up and out of the bedroom. I couldn't help Nate by lying alone in bed with my tail between my legs.

"Why don't you boys stop by the gas station today?" my mother suggested brightly. "Even if he's not working, his coworkers may know where he's staying and give you the address."

"We could...." From the tone of his voice, Zander seemed to be on the fence about that.

"Or you could just wait some more." My father voiced our other option. "Maybe you'll hear from him in time."

We all stared at Dad.

"Or not," he added, again putting words to our thoughts.

"We have to try to find him so we can discuss this situation. We can find out how Cindy is and what the two of them are going to do next." I was trying to stay rational, but I knew that, in order to discuss anything with Nate, we had to actually find him.

"Didn't you say they have an aunt who lives just outside of Boston? Maybe Cindy could live there?" Mom then added something we, too, had long been curious about. "And why was this aunt absent for the past three plus years, since Nate's mother was incarcerated?"

"Nate told us that his mom and her sister hadn't had any contact in years. Her brother, Rich, was the only person in the family she kept in touch with. So, when the kids needed a place to go, he was the person Nate's mother contacted," Zander explained.

"Does Nate's aunt know what has been going on behind closed doors?"

"I know Nate wouldn't have told her. And I really doubt Cindy brought it up."

"But Zander, Nate told us he was going to ask her about the possibility of Cindy finishing high school living with her aunt and cousin. I'm pretty sure he planned on sending money for the next four years to Terri, that's his aunt's name, to help support Cindy. He probably would have had to explain in that conversation the reasons she wasn't safe here with her uncle."

My father got up and approached me. "That Nate is a very good boy, and he's very considerate of his sister. Try to keep in mind that he's not behaving rationally right now. He blames himself for what's happened to Cindy. He's suffering with guilt and doesn't know where to turn. Nate probably believes he doesn't deserve comfort."

Dad was trying to help us understand where our boyfriend was coming from and why he hadn't gotten in touch with us. "Dad, I've been hurt before, and I know that a hurting heart doesn't always act in its own best interest." My father was right.

Dad smiled. "I don't want to see you boys become desperate in your effort to reach Nate. I—"

"Mr. Minton, with all due respect, it's as if each of us is *alone* when we don't have Nate. There is no 'us' without the three of us."

I nodded in agreement. "Dad, you're talking to two people who are brokenhearted. Our relationship started as three friends, and it grew as three. It won't just become two because one of us is missing. Without our third, I'm nothing more than Zander's friend."

My parents looked at each other, clearly confused. They didn't understand that the unique and precious quality of our relationship came from the essence of our three-ness. The trust, love, and sharing that we'd grown to cherish had evolved from three different young men fitting together in a specific way that could not be replicated by just two.

My gaze met Zander's, and we both nodded. My parents, our friends, the whole world might not understand, but we knew that we were three or we were over. Thankfully, my parents were only confused and not repulsed or angered by our stance on the matter.

"Well, then, I suppose you boys need to find Nate."

On second thought, it seemed as if Mom got the picture.

"I miss Natey-nate," said Lola looking up from her cards.

"Where is big ol' Nate?" Sarah was genuinely baffled.

I took Sarah's chubby hand in mine and replied, "That's what we're going to figure out."

zanderZ@catchme.com

I called off the One Voice meeting tonight, Dan. Just plain old couldn't cope with it. Saturday night changed a lot of things for me and Casey, not to mention Nate. And I'm hoping it doesn't ultimately change my commitment to the things I've come to believe in. But I'm not ready to think that far ahead. I'm crushed and I'm in pain and I'm not ready to lead a group devoted to anything. No matter how vital the cause.

I LEFT our dormitory room in the afternoon today, as I think both Casey and I needed some time to be alone after what went down with Nate last night. And shit, it's been twenty-four hours. If I don't spell it out to you now, I may just stuff it deep inside myself and hold it there forever.

I'm sitting here in the lower campus laundry room, of all places. And since it's a Sunday night, I figured the place would be all kinds of packed—full of upperclassmen getting their supply of clean clothes for the week. But it's empty, except for me and my laptop, perched on an orange plastic chair in the corner, and a girl I recognize from the library, who's washing enough clothes to outfit an army. It must be her turn to wash, dry, and fold the clothes of everybody in her apartment.

Looking for Nate, Casey and I made two trips to the gas station. The first time we just drove in, saw a guy we didn't know working the pumps, and pulled right back out. The second time, about an hour later, the same guy was working the pumps, so we parked and went inside the minimart. Nate's friend Missy was working at the cash register. At least she fit his general description of his friend Missy—"sorta tall, with dark hair that looks kinda stiff in the front, and always chompin' on bubble gum."

Missy was a fucking fountain of knowledge.

"Oh, shit. Yeah. I know exactly where the guy is staying." She gloated for a couple minutes and then pronounced, "The guy's staying on my couch."

That news was unexpected.

"Nate told me that his uncle got hauled into the slammer for some shit or another, and he lost his house. His uncle hadn't paid rent in a while, and the landlord took advantage of the opportunity to kick Nate to the curb."

That explained the bare house and the for-rent signs.

"If you guys wanna see him, though, you can stop by my apartment. No prob."

Casey's eyes got all wide, and he started nodding. I thought he might jump outta his skin. "Could you jot down your address and we'll head over and see him?"

She tore off a piece of a brown paper bag and wrote down an address that was actually in the same complex as Ma's, but way down at the other end. "If you wanna see him smile, bring beer." I took the scrap of paper from her.

Nate hadn't indulged in booze or a joint or anything else since we'd become friends with him. This didn't sound good.

We didn't say even one fucking word to each other in the car. I think we both already knew what was coming was gonna suck royally. And it was gonna change things.

When we got there, Nate let us into a dingy, smoky, crack-house kind of apartment. It stunk like stale cigarette smoke. The walls were all brown with stains and a bunch of skinny, stray-looking cats were draped all over the furniture. Nate didn't even wait for us to close the door. He just turned around and walked across the room, and then dropped his ass smack dab in the middle of the couch. He sat there squinting at us, wearing nothing but a wifebeater tank top and unzipped jeans.

Nate looked like shit. He smelled like shit. And he appeared very relaxed and at home in this pile-of-shit apartment. From the looks of him, he hadn't shaved or brushed his hair in days. This scene reminded me a lot of when we first saw Casey after he'd been beaten by Liz Trainer. It was a gross and nasty sight. It spelled major depression.

We weren't offered a seat or a beer, which was what he was drinking. Nate's dark, dull eyes found the television set as if we weren't there.

"Dude." Yeah, that was my brilliant opening. "Dude, where have you been?"

"Eh?"

I knew he'd heard exactly what I'd asked, but I repeated myself nonetheless. "You fell off the edge of the fucking earth, dude. You never told us how Cindy was or what happened to Rich or where the fuck you've been."

Nate looked at me. Directly. Angrily. Scarily. "So here's the deal. Rich tried to choke Cindy to death while I was frolicking in the grassy quad with you guys, in a fucked-up effort to encourage all the poor homos at Boston City College to get the hell outta their closets. Sorry I inconvenienced ya by not callin' every five fuckin' minutes."

Casey took a step behind me, but still he managed to squeak out his question. "Is Cindy all right?"

Nate looked at Casey. "I don't know, babe. But I do know that she couldn't talk for a week, she's *still* having trouble swallowin', and her skinny neck is covered in bruises and scratches from her own fingers trying to claw my uncle's hands off her. Oh, and she pissed her pants when the ass hat was stranglin' her. From what Aunt Terri tells me, it was a lovely scene, top to bottom. So I would say she's not doin' too good."

"Any permanent injuries?" I asked hesitantly. This was like walking on a pile of broken glass. It was really hard to know where to step.

"It's hard to say. Psychological trauma kinda sticks with ya, don't it, Casey?" I had asked the question, but he glared at Casey as he replied. His voice was low, smooth, and cool. I could not detect a hint of emotion in it, even when he said, "Plus, Cindy won't see me. Don't wanna lay her eyes on the brother who screwed her life up so fuckin' bad." Then he directed his icy glare toward me again. "She's let Aunt Terri in her confidence, though, and Terri keeps me up to date on the fucked-up status of Cindy's trauma."

There was silence in the room, with the exception of various feline mewls from the small gang of cats that seemed to be stalking Casey and me. It was a heavy, uncomfortable silence. A profound silence. A silence that told me things I didn't want to hear or know.

"Anyhow, I got booted from my house, cuz good ole Uncle Rich is in the slammer now, where he belongs. And I can't pay for that shithole on my own. Lucky for me I got friends like Missy, who'll take me in for a price."

Nate had never said so much in so short a time period since we'd met him.

"I ain't paid the price yet. It's fuckin' steep."

I had a feeling I knew exactly what was on the *price tag*—to keep Missy satisfied in bed. I sincerely hoped Casey was clueless about it.

"But it'll surely come down to me payin' that price—sooner rather than later. Missy ain't too patient. So, in answer to your question, 'where you been, Nate?' I been around. Kickin' around. But I been real fuckin' busy. I been tryin' to get my sister to look at me. I been talkin' to the cops about my asshole uncle. Been movin' my crap outta one shithole and into another. Been pumpin' gas into lazy drivers' tanks. Like I said, been busy."

Casey and I stared as Nate slid his venomous gaze away from my face to look at the television.

"That's where I been."

Casey must have felt brave or something. He stepped over to that nasty couch. Really cautiously, as if he weren't sure whether or not Nate was gonna bite him, he sat on the edge of the couch and tried to take Nate's hand. But Nate snatched it away.

"Sweetheart... um, Nate, what's going on with us? You haven't answered our calls or texts or—"

"Shit, kid. Ain't it obvious?" Nate actually smiled. "It's over with us three. A done fuckin' deal." Still smiling, he stared straight ahead. "Can't you dudes take a fuckin' hint? Nah. S'pose I gotta spell it out for ya."

Casey's eyes filled with tears, and I moved to him quickly and placed my hands firmly on his shoulders.

But Nate wasn't done with us. "Now you two *college boys* can concentrate on gettin' smart and changin' the friggin' world so three homos like us can fuck each other without no public interference."

I opened my mouth to challenge him, but I closed it just as quickly. There would be no discussion today. This Nate wasn't the Nate we knew.

Instead I took Casey by the arm and helped him stand up. Tears were flowing pretty freely down Casey's face now, and he looked like he was in shock. I figured he'd have a full-blown panic attack soon. How could Nate hurt Casey like this? He knew how soft, sweet, and vulnerable Casey was. "We'll get outta your hair, then, dude."

For an instant, and I'm talking about a fraction of a second, I thought I saw a flash of pain cross Nate's face. But he quickly caught himself and said in a sarcastic tone, "Au revoir."

It was ironic that he chose to say his final good-bye to us in French, as we'd fallen in love through the completion of a French project during our junior year in high school. Then he said it again. "Au-fuckin'-revoir."

I led Casey to the apartment door, and we went outside. Casey lost it by the time we got to the car. A full-on anxiety attack hit him hard. He had to do regulated breathing techniques the whole way back to his house, but thankfully he didn't barf.

SO, DAN, that's how shit went down with Nate, pretty much exactly. Right after that, Casey said he wanted to go back to school. I don't think he wanted to subject his family to his oncoming depression. We didn't talk about anything 'til Sunday morning, when we decided that Casey and I would put our romantic relationship on the back burner. We both hung around the dorm room until Casey went off to the library. I decided to get the hell outta that room before he came back.

We don't know how to act together anymore. This platonic relationship is new to us. We need to talk a lot more to make it work, but it isn't the right time.

Never noticed how friggin' tiny that dormitory room was before today.

Z

17

NATE'S DIARY

October 25

AIN'T WRITTEN here in a hell of a long while. Like maybe two weeks or so.

Couldn't do it. Couldn't make myself sit down and write about what was goin' on inside my fucked-up head. Kinda wanted to, a whole bunch of times. Thought that maybe if I just sat my ass down and got some shit offa my chest, then maybe I could read it back to myself out loud and make some sense of it.

But every time I picked up the notebook, grabbed a pen, found a place to park my truck where I could be alone with my thoughts for a bit, somethin' stopped me from writin'.

I finally figured out that I don't wanna get my head clear on things. I don't *wanna* get the whys and the hows of what'd happened to my life and then respond to it like a man. Nope. What I want to do is to run. To steer clear. To do everythin' in my power to make sure that nobody can wreck me again, the way Cindy'd just done.

And lemme tell ya, I am fuckin' scared stupid by how much I love Casey and Zander.

Am I mad at 'em for distractin' me from Cindy, leadin' her to gettin' the beatin' of her life? Well, yeah. I'm pissed off at them two, 'specially Zander for sendin' me on a guilt trip about leavin' before his super important One Voice rally. But I'm pissed off at them two for way more than temptin' me away from my responsibility to Cindy. I'm mad as hell cuz their lives are movin' on in ways that mine just can't. I'm stuck in a rut, waitin' for Cindy to graduate from high school and be old enough to leave our hell home. I'm pissed cuz I kept on takin' beatin' after beatin' so she didn't have to. Don't know how that's Casey and Zander's fault, but somehow, in the back of my mind, it just is.

I felt like them two left me. And I'm here alone.

We aren't "us three" no more. They're "them two," and I'm all alone, way the fuck up here. Alone like always. Watchin' out for Cindy. Gettin' pummeled by my Uncle. Workin' my ass off at stupid jobs I don't give a shit about.

When they walked outta Missy's place last Saturday, I felt slapped upside the head all over again. Watched 'em out the window as they walked to Miz Minton's Volvo, Casey fightin' a panic attack. Yeah, that made me feel lower than low. And Zander was supportin' his every step. All I kept sayin' to myself was, "Them two, not me. Them two, not me."

Wah-fuckin'-wah. Looks like it's time for Nate-the-asshole's pity party.

Guess I don't have to worry no more about them two forgettin' all about me and not bein' "us three" no more. I fixed that, didn't I? Treated them two like the lowly shit I know *I am*. Meant to drive 'em off, and I did.

Can't live this broken-apart life no more. Can't make them two live it with me.

Thing is, it's all so much friggin' easier to deal with when I'm drunk and high.

zanderZ@catchme.com

Life is sucking to the max, Dan.

Thank Christ I have Claire and Anna and you to vent on otherwise my marbles would be rolling down the street. Had lunch with the girls today at New Caf. Didn't wanna risk bumping into Casey on upper campus, because, man, he's down low, as in superdepressed, and I needed a chance to come up for air.

We just shot the shit at lunch, talking about indie bands and YouTube. But at the end of lunch, Claire went out on a limb and asked, "So you canceled One Voice last Sunday. Didn't see that coming. What's up?"

And I answered her. I just fucking answered honestly. "Me and Nate and Casey, we sorta...." It was damn hard to make myself say the words. "We sorta broke up."

The girls gawked at me for a second. Then they exchanged a quick glance, and Claire nodded to Anna in a "take it away, Anna" way, like these kinds of situations were her territory.

"Shit, dude. That sucks." Anna grabbed her mass of light brown hair, pulled it all to one side, and started checking the bottom for split ends or something. "Mind sharing with us what happened? I mean, what led to that."

"Because you three seemed so solid and in love and...." Claire's voice trailed away just like Anna's had.

I only had to think about whether I was gonna spill the details for about two seconds. I needed to get some heavy stuff off my chest. "Remember when Casey and Nate and I split from the Coming Out Day rally, like all of a sudden? And you know how I called and asked you two to cover for me because I couldn't come back?"

The girls nodded.

I went on to tell them the whole story about Cindy getting assaulted, choked nearly to death, and then the details of Nate's ugly home life. I told them how Casey and I had sat by and watched— hoping things would be different and even encouraging him to make changes—but how neither of us had ever put a foot down and said, "No more."

"How did that lead to you breaking up?" Anna asked.

"Nate fell off the face of the earth after what happened with Cindy. When he left that day, we never heard from him again. He never answered our calls or texts. So Casey and I went home last weekend. We tracked him down, and when we found him, he said he was done with us. Just done."

"You're kidding."

"Anna, I *so* wouldn't kid you about this."

She nodded. "What did you guys do to change his mind?"

It was my turn to shrug. "We didn't do anything to change his mind. I could see that Casey was having a meltdown and that Nate had dug his heels in. No good was gonna come of it if we stuck around and begged. So I just hung on to Casey for dear life and escorted him out the door." I felt like a loser, admitting that I'd cut and run on Nate with such apparent ease. But I knew Nate, and the timing had been wrong to have any kind of civil discussion with him.

Claire leaned forward and examined my face closely. "Now what are you gonna do?"

"Don't know, at this point. But I have two problems. There's the whole Nate issue, and there's also the fact that Casey and I are broken up too."

"But why does it have to be over with him? You and Casey don't have any problems."

That was a very good question and one that needed answering. We had all agreed that we were a threesome. If one person was out, our relationship was invalid. Maybe it was, but Casey and I needed to discuss the situation in depth.

I doubt that a throuple—and particularly one that worked so well—can be downsized to a twosome and stay alive.

That's my story. I'm sticking with it. Even though it sucks donkey balls.

Zan

CASEY'S REAL LIFE

ZANDER AND I finally sat down to have a discussion about him and me. He was the one to initiate the discussion, as I had absolutely no clue what to do next. As in, no clue whatsoever.

Zander took me to a diner about a thirty-minute subway ride away from campus so we wouldn't be distracted while we talked.

But it was Halloween weekend, so instead of being distracted by college students, we were distracted by families with adorable children in costumes. They reminded me of how Zander, Nate, and I had taken Lola and Sarah trick-or-treating the year before. They had dressed as Lilo and Stitch. That evening was now nothing but a painful memory.

"We gotta talk about this, Casey."

I looked at Zander over my vanilla shake. "I know we do."

"I hope we haven't lost him, like, forever. And that when Cindy's better and she's settled in a new home, he'll be calm enough to think this over and realize how much we love him." Zander seemed pretty confident.

"I hope so." I was not in top chatterbox form.

"But we still have to figure out what we are to each other until then."

"Or if that ever happens," I pointed out.

"That's a possibility we have to consider."

My chest tightened.

"Sip your shake." Zander knew my mouth got dry when I was anxious. "Go ahead. Take a drink."

I sipped my shake through my straw while gazing into Zander's eyes, in an effort to absorb some of his emotional strength. Because Zander was the strong one, the well-adjusted one, and the most "normal" guy in our former group of three. I needed Zander's strength and love and support.

"I can't lose you, Zander. I still love you... so much." My chest tightened a bit more as I uttered my traitorous thought. I struggled to inhale.

Zander smiled, but it was a sad smile. "I don't want to lose you either, Casey."

"And... and if Nate comes back to us, he needs an "us" to come back to, right?" I knew I sounded hopeful and that maybe I was also grasping at straws.

Zander reached across the table to take my upturned hand in his. When I felt his warm palm pressed against mine, I knew it was right that we stuck together.

"I don't want to give up on him. I mean, I think he needs some time to deal with Cindy's injuries, and probably the guilt that he feels over her being attacked when he was away from her, here with us. But I think we need to prove to him that we're still here for him and that—"

"Casey." Zander interrupted me. "Let's not overwhelm him any further right now. We need to take things slowly. Like, for example, let's not call him any time soon. That's too direct and in your face. Instead let's text him every few days and let him know that we're still thinking of him. That we're still here for him."

He was right. "Okay. Maybe you should be in charge of when we contact him. I might be a little bit overeager."

Zander squeezed my hand to let me know he agreed. And then we were served our burgers and fries.

"You need to eat that whole burger, dude."

Zander had noticed my recent weight loss. It was just so hard for me to eat when my life was crumbling around me.

But I nodded dutifully and picked up the burger with both hands. I said, "I want to wait on... I mean, do you mind if we wait for a while on being intimate? You know, on having sex... without Nate?"

"Of course we can. There's no rush on that stuff."

I took a minute to study Zander's face as he bit into his burger. He was handsome in a Justin-Bieber-without-an-attitude way. He was cool, cute, preppy, and just clean cut enough to make girls and guys look his way. And Zander was still mine, and he was going to be patient with me. I was lucky to have him, and I knew it, but the other half of my heart ached for what it had lost.

18
NATE'S DIARY

October 31

GOT FRIGGIN' toasted last night—and the night before that and probably the one before that too. But who the fuck is countin'? Cindy sure ain't countin' the days 'til she sees her big bro again, that's for fuckin' sure. She won't even say no quick hello to me on my cell.

Called Aunt Terri's house last night, hopin' like hell that Cindy'd talk to me. Imagine my surprise when she answered Terri's cell phone. I was like, "Cindy, I'm sorry. I fucked up major league and I know it."

Know what Cindy said? She said, "Your little sister is dead to you, Nate. She's gone for good. Her uncle choked the life out of her when her brother didn't come home from his fuckfest weekend with his boyfriends." Then Cindy ended the phone call, but not before she told me to leave her the hell alone. I was friggin' crushed.

And then there's Casey and Zander. Sure, they still text me now and again, but I don't give a shit about that. I *can't* give a shit. I let them two go, and I'm glad I did.

It's like I'm just plain pissed off. Don't know who at. Just pissed and can't be bothered no more.

Can't be bothered with talkin' sweet to them guys. Can't be bothered makin' promises I ain't no good at keepin'. Won't be put out by them two no more.

Not that givin' a shit about them two was ever some kinda chore.

Cuz it wasn't.

I ain't got time to think on this no more. It's Halloween, right? Time to party.

zanderZ@catchme.com

D—

I'm fucking everything up here at school, man. I just can't concentrate on studying, let alone on planning agendas for One Voice meetings. My grades are starting to suck. I'm afraid I might lose my merit scholarship if I keep going like this. And I've canceled the past two One Voice meetings because I just can't deal with it.

I'm *not* rising to meet the challenge. No. This fucked-up situation is proving that I'm weak and lost and scared and I can't handle shit. Then I remember what Casey and Nate have been through in their lives, and I say to myself, "Cowboy up, dude."

You know, bro, when I knock away all of the guilt and loneliness and worry that's dragging me under, I realize I *have* experienced a huge loss. Casey and Nate and I were like a family for the past year and a half, Dan. Shit. It was almost two years, really. And you were gone, and you know the story with Ma and her flavor of the week boyfriend. I had *nobody* back home 'til they came along.

And Casey's acting like everything's just super fucking rosy—which we both know it's not—and he's filled with more energy than ever.

"Morning, Zander. Want to go for a run before breakfast? I feel like I've been studying nonstop, and I need a break for fresh air and exercise."

Hello. Casey Minton—*a run*? Not normal. Not normal at all. Well, not for Casey, our sweet bookworm.

My lifesavers have been Anna and Claire. I was gonna cancel One Voice again this week, but, like I said, they saved me.

We were sitting at New Caf on lower campus. It's kind of my sanctuary from all other freshmen, and maybe even a little bit from Casey, because things are not flowing naturally between us. So there we were, eating lunch together—the fries are stellar—and I just came out and said it.

"I can't handle the whole One Voice thing right now. My frigging life is falling apart and... and I just don't have the motivation."

When I said that, Anna and Claire exchanged one of their all-knowing glances. Whenever a complicated issue arises, Claire's dark eyes shift automatically to Anna's light ones, and then she tilts her head as if to say "You take this one." It reminds me of the way Casey, Nate, and I used to be able to communicate without words.

Well, that's a done deal, so there's no point dwelling on it, is there?

Anna piped up with, "Let us help out."

Claire nodded. "If you cancel again, we'll lose the few followers we have."

I liked the way she said "we," as if I wasn't in this thing alone. So I said, "You're right. You're totally right."

"From this point forward, the three of us will run it together. What's on the agenda?"

"Um...." The three of us. The words "the three of us" echoed in my head, reminding me of Casey and Nate and what no longer existed between us. "I had planned for One Voice to give back to the community by sponsoring a food drive. I thought maybe we could work out the details."

"Awesome idea. The food can be collected in time for Thanksgiving."

Thanksgiving... without Nate coming over to Casey's house and eating turkey wraps with stuffing and cranberry sauce, like we did on our very first ever date.

"Let's bring some community maps, and we can divide up the campus apartments and surrounding neighborhoods. We'll give everyone who attends the meeting an area to cover."

"We need One Voice T-shirts to wear while we do community work. I know this guy—he can make them really cheap. I'll get right on that today," Claire offered.

"Do you have a logo that you usually use?" Anna was right beside her, making this happen.

The girls were refusing to allow me to wallow in my despair. And One Voice was the best distraction. "Yeah. In high school this super-artsy student designed a logo with a rainbow and a bunch of sort of stick people singing, with the words 'One Voice.'"

"Get me a copy, and I'll give it to my friend and…."

And so, my life goes on.

My life goes on—without Nate.

Bummed to the max, but I'm surviving.

Z

CASEY'S REAL LIFE

I WAS running on empty. But in order to survive Nate leaving us, I had to keep busy. I'd taken up running, which shocked Zander. Anything to *keep moving* so I didn't have to think. And it was something Zander and I could do together without discussing our situation. We couldn't very easily run and talk simultaneously— well, at least *I* couldn't.

It was exactly four weeks since Nate had last been part of our relationship. Zander and I had just returned from our morning run. Zander was showering, and I was lying on my bed with nothing to do but think.

I was comfortable with thinking about Advanced Biology and Inside US History and Freshman Lit. And I was fine when I was running or helping Zander with One Voice plans or shopping online, even. But I was not okay when I stopped, because then I'd think about Nate.

Which was dangerous territory.

Note to self. Casey, do anything but think of Nate.

As I was scrambling to find something to distract me from dwelling on him, Zander came back from the shower. One white towel was wrapped around his waist, and he was rubbing his shaggy wet hair with another. He looked pretty good. Add to that my loneliness, my neediness, the fact that we hadn't been in bed together to cuddle in a while, let alone to make love. I jumped on him.

"Hey, hey. Casey, what's gotten into you, babe?"

Nate always called me babe.

Zander lifted my face to his. I could see in his eyes that he was hungry for closeness, for affection, for comfort—for me. He bent down and took my lips with a passion I'd missed.

"Casey, uh…." Zander's breathing was husky. "The bed. Let's go lie down."

He pulled me to his bed, then pushed me down on my back and climbed on top of me.

"Zander, I've missed you… so much."

Before I knew it, we were kissing passionately, grinding our hips together.

"I want you," Zander uttered, his hands on my gym shorts, tugging them down.

"I haven't showered yet, Zander."

He replied quickly, "I don't care."

My shorts were soon around my ankles, and my briefs had joined them. "Oh, I need you." My hands made quick work of that towel. It dropped to the floor beside the bed.

The T-shirt I wore was soon on the floor beside the towel, and it looked like we were in business. I couldn't begin to describe the bliss of feeling his soft lips on my chest. It was as if I had never been touched before. I writhed and moaned beneath him. When his tongue stretched out to taste my nipple and the warm moistness started to take me apart, piece by piece, I pulled Zander's head to my chest, and then I reached out for Nate.

I reached out for Nate.

"Nate." I said it. Out loud. And everything stopped.

Zander flopped back on the bed, and I flipped on top of him so I was draped across his chest. And we both cried.

Even Zander—strong, controlled, reasonable Zander—shed tears on that bed.

We missed the rest of our classes that day. It didn't matter because we needed so badly to just lie in each other's arms. I think we both knew that we weren't going to last another day if we didn't inhale each other's breath and profess our love aloud in the midst of this trying circumstance.

"Nate has nobody." We had both been silent for the better part of an hour when I finally spoke. "He's alone, Zander."

"I know." He sniffed a couple times, and I recognized pain in the tone of his voice.

"Think he still needs us?" I asked.

He hesitated, and I thought he was going to shrug, but instead he nodded. Just once. "I think he probably does."

"Feelings… you know, deep feelings like ours. They don't just disappear into thin air, do they?" I needed to hear him say no, but he just shook his head several times. "Can we go and try to see him again? I want to see him, Zander. I can't do this anymore." That was my cue to start crying again. "I just can't *do* this any… anymore."

"Let's wait, Casey, just a little bit longer." He sounded incredibly certain.

"He's going to forget all about us." I was so worried that I admitted my greatest fear.

Zander took my face in his hands and looked me right in the eyes. "He could *never* forget about you—no one could." He looked at me with so much love and sureness, I thought he could be right.

Maybe, just maybe, what he was saying could be true.

"I love you, Zander. And I want you too. But I think we can wait for a while… for making love. And we can wait a little longer to go find Nate."

"We can. But I can't express to you exactly how much I'd like to put my new lovemaking skills to work on you. I hadn't even had a chance to practice everything I learned when I was cut off." He looked down at my face with a crooked grin.

I had to laugh at that, because I knew just what he meant. "And the feeling is totally mutual." But we could wait a bit longer.

It wasn't all about sex.

It was, however, still all about the three of us. Until that was no longer the case, making love didn't fit into the equation.

19
NATE'S DIARY

November 9

STILL TRYIN' to figure out how I got myself into this fine pile of steamin' shit… and neck deep in it. Cuz at the moment, I ain't got no place to live. Looks like I'm gonna be campin' out in my truck.

It's not that I don't have no money. I got some—not a lot. Up until the shit hit the fan, I was spendin' most of my cash on payin' my share to Uncle Rich for livin' in his house, and spendin' much of the rest on takin' care of Cindy. Cuz a girl can't live on mac and cheese. If Cindy was gonna have herself an apple to eat, I was gonna have to be the one buyin' it. What I wouldn't give to have those days back—but those days are gone.

So, I have a small bit of money, but not enough for a security deposit and first and last month's rent. Just don't got it—don't got nowhere to get it neither. Looks like I'm gonna have to start savin', and that'll be a challenge if I don't cut out some of the booze and weed—which I don't see happenin' no time soon, seein' as they're my only reasons for livin'.

Had it made stayin' with Missy 'til last night, when I more or less got my ass kicked outta her place. But I just couldn't do what she wanted me to do. Thought I could. Let her think I could—which turned out to be my biggest mistake. But when push came to shove, man, I just couldn't fuck her.

Missy'd been hintin' at us gettin' busy in the sack since day one. And I mean "Day One," as in back when I started workin' at the gas station when I was still with Casey and Zander. So, last night, when we both had a night off work together and then got drunk and stoned, we found ourselves in her bed. It didn't come as no major surprise that she expected me to fuck her. Shit, it shoulda been simple as wham, bam... you know the rest. It woulda been kinda like payin' the rent. I didn't *wanna* do her, but it was the cost of sleepin' on that crappy couch.

Thing is, when push came to shove, I just couldn't fuck her. I'm not sayin' it was cuz of Casey and Zander. Them two aren't mine no more. But I couldn't fuck her. No more on that subject, 'cept for the fact that I'm kicked outta her place now.

So I'm real thankful for my coat and my fleece blanket. And tomorrow, after work, I'll invest in a good sleepin' bag. It's not like it's January or nothin'. It's only early November, and it really ain't that cold. I can just turn the truck on and blast the heat whenever I my ass starts freezin' off.

They got a shower at the garage, and if I time it right at work, I can grab a shower there sometimes.

This'll be cool for a while.

Yeah. This'll work okay 'til I can save up some cash.

zanderZ @ catchme.com

Hey, dude.

Almost entered today's post on my blog spot. Yeah, as in, the One Voice blog spot. And nah, I'm not doing too much better in regard to Nate being MIA. Or about Nate having dumped our asses, which is the plain truth. Casey and I are still suffering, still depressed, still feeling like when we're just the two of us, something is missing.

But I have to get some stuff done, you know, bro? First off, I still have a lot to learn on sexuality/gender issues, so I'm gonna have our group watch a video that was recommended to me by a guy in my ethics class, called *Ending Gender* by Scott Turner Schofield. If One Voice doesn't understand the issue, nobody will, right? I'm hurt and pissed about my personal stuff, but I've rededicated myself to the cause. And so has Casey. It helps keep our minds off the bullshit.

On Sunday night, Casey and I are gonna arrive at the meeting with two huge trash bags of buttered popcorn, and Anna and Claire have the drinks covered. After we watch the video, we'll talk as a group about shredding labels. We can brainstorm about how to reach everybody in the school with our message of welcome and acceptance, so no one feels left out because of their sexual orientation or gender identity.

That's what's up in my neck of the woods, dude.

Super stoked to hear that you and Abby are heading east for Thanksgiving. It's gonna be like a real *holiday* at the Zane home, and I use that term loosely.

Keep cool.

Z-man

CASEY'S REAL LIFE

"WE'RE GOING home for Thanksgiving weekend, and Zander says we can stop by Missy's apartment and check on Nate if we haven't heard from him by then." My chest actually got tight, the way it usually did at the beginning of a panic attack, every time I thought about seeing Nate. But this time, I started right into a series of deep breaths to stop the dry mouth and nausea before I fell into a full-blown episode.

"You think he would ever agree to celebrate Thanksgiving with either one of your families?" Claire asked with honest and hopeful sincerity. I really wanted to say yes. But I had serious doubts that he would so much as open the door to us.

Zander answered, "We'll certainly invite him. That's all I know. But we aren't really in charge of his response to the invitation." Zander stopped, thought for a minute, and then reached beside him to take my hand beneath the table at College Pizza. "Casey and I don't really know this new version of Nate DeMarco."

Anna and Claire sat across from us, also holding hands, their brows sporting identical worry wrinkles. They had become our other half, in a sense. Zander and I met them almost daily for lunch or dinner, we'd seen several movies with them, and we recently started planning One Voice meetings as a group. More importantly, we confided in them. They knew the full extent of the bullying I suffered at Benjamin Franklin High School. All of it. They were aware of Nate's violent home life, and they knew the maternal neglect that Zander had long endured. And the sharing wasn't a one-way street. Zander and I knew about their struggles with their Christian identities and how hiding their relationship had taken a toll on them, individually and as a couple.

They were our true friends. Other than Nate and Zander, they were the first friends I'd ever had. A rush of warmth enveloped my heart, and naturally, as I *am* Casey Minton, my eyes filled with tears.

Anna practically climbed over the table in an effort to touch me, to comfort me. "Honey, we don't have to talk about Nate anymore if it upsets you. Sorry. Oh, I'm so sorry."

"No... no, Anna. Don't be sorry, please." I wiped my eyes with my paper napkin. "The tears are sort of.... They're happy tears."

All three of my dining companions gawked at me, probably thinking, "Happy tears? Casey's finally lost his marbles."

"I'm not happy about Nate being gone. It's not that at all." I stopped talking long enough to take a calming breath and dab at my eyes with the napkin one more time. "It's just, I was thinking that you two are my first real true friends, other than Zander and Nate."

Suddenly our corner booth at the pizza parlor was a cryfest— the exact opposite of a lovefest. All four of us were wiping our eyes.

Anna headed toward the bathroom. "I'm afraid I'm not into public displays of *emotion*. But for the record, I'm fine with PDAs." She made an attempt to laugh. "Order me a cannoli—a chocolate chip one if they have them today. Needing chocolate to swing my mood back up."

That left Claire, who sat opposite Zander and me, her dark eyes wide and wet. "I haven't had many friends in my life either, Casey," she confided quietly. "So you're both very special to me. And if I had one wish, it would be that our little foursome will turn into a fivesome."

It suddenly hit me that Nate would love these two friends of ours, and I smiled. But the smile fell off my face as I wondered if he'd ever have a chance to get to know them.

20
Nate's Diary

November 17

SICK AGAIN. Had to work last night, though, seein' as I missed the day before yesterday and a couple days last week. Got myself a stern warnin' from the boss man. He was like, "If you can't get your sorry ass to those gas pumps, I'll find some loser who can."

Last week I fucked up and missed work cuz I was hungover and couldn't even get my ass outta the truck. Thank Christ I got me a good hidin' spot for the truck, down near the lake, cuz I couldn't of dealt with movin' it on those nights. Messed up thing is, before I was with Casey and Zander, I used to take girls to this spot to smoke weed, drink beer, and suck face. And when us three were real needy for each other senior year, I even took Casey and Zander to this spot. We'd park and have ourselves a bit of fun. Nah, that ain't true. We mostly just held each other in my truck—us three lined up across the bench seat, little Casey 'tween me and Zander. Little did I know I was gonna be callin' this clearin' under the pine trees home sweet fuckin' home in a short year.

I think I'd be doin' good if I could get rid of this hackin' cough. Yesterday I had chills and shit, but either I'm gettin' used to them or they went away altogether. Can't say which it is.

Good thing is, I don't have no time to think about them two down in Boston. Nope.

And not thinkin' about them is just fine by me.

One more thing. I quit the dog walkin' gig. Too fuckin' much for me to handle on an empty belly and not enough sleep.

But I gotta keep what I got goin' at the gas station, or I'll be flat broke. Time to head to work.

zanderZ@catchme.com

Danny—

Once again, I almost posted on the One Voice blog spot, because some of what I'm gonna tell you is good stuff for the blog. See, man, what we did as a group—I'm talking about the BCC One Voice Club—was monumental. So we have like twenty members now, right? Well, get this—according to the food pantry, our twenty members collected more canned and nonperishable food than an entire South Shore middle school.

Teamwork, right?

Yeah, we got teamwork down—especially me, Casey, Anna, and Claire. After our One Voice meeting on Sunday night, where we collected the cans from the members and then watched a music video of this band called Rise Against doing the song "Make It Stop (September's Children)" that showed all of this nasty bullying at school. These three kids on the video seriously contemplate suicide, even go so far as to almost do it, but then something stops them, and you see flashes of the future they'll have because they hung on through that incredibly hard moment. I showed it because it has video clips of all these kids and young adults saying that things will get better in life.

So the above was the part that was suitable for the One Voice blog.

I WATCHED Casey closely while the video played. He knew I was gonna show it at the meeting, and we'd watched it a few times in our room so the topic didn't take him by surprise. But I knew the bullying topic hit real close to home, and I didn't take my eyes off him. I wished like hell Nate were there to hold him close while we watched and during the discussion that followed. At times like Sunday night, Casey needed the feeling of protection that Nate inspired. Nate—solid, tough, burly—would do his damnedest to make both of us feel safe. And we did, when he was around, which is the key phrase.

The dude isn't around.

So the job fell to me.

And I wasn't doing a very good job. At the One Voice meeting, I failed epically. I just watched him. I didn't hold him or even go to him. I was kinda frozen in place.

To make up for it, I tried to be extra attentive afterward, when we got back to the room. At about midnight, I thought I heard a sniffle, and I knew Casey was upset. So I pulled myself from my bed, stepped across the room, and stood beside him. "Can I get in with you?"

Casey slid over so he was against the wall and pulled back the covers for me.

As soon as I was under the covers, I drew Casey down against my chest and held him. He felt so small, and real fragile too. He was shuddering. I knew he was fighting back sobs.

"I c-can't d-do this much longer, Z-Zander...."

I knew what he was talking about... and I knew he was right. Because I couldn't love Nate from afar, hope he'd see the light, and wonder if he was okay for very much longer either. Casey and I weren't really living. We were just waiting.

And living life for what would maybe come tomorrow, or maybe next week, or maybe not ever, wasn't working for us. It wasn't healthy for either me or Casey.

Casey must have confused my silence for disagreement, because he started explaining himself. "It hurts too much not to know if we'll ever see him... and hold him and love him again."

I smoothed the soft skin of his shaking back and slid my fingertips slowly up and down his spine. "Don't worry, Casey. I can't keep doing this either."

Casey's body stiffened in surprise.

"If he won't see us or talk to us this weekend, I think we need to move on."

It was as if someone had lit a fire on the soles of his feet. He jumped—or maybe lurched up—so he was kneeling beside me on the bed. "You're going to move on—without me?"

I felt like someone had kicked me in the gut. Just the simple thought of leaving Casey did that to me. "No—no, of course not."

He still didn't relax. "Y-you said m-move on...." His voice was weak, a mere whisper.

"*We* need to move on, Casey. If Nate refuses to see us, or talk to us, or if we can't find him, *we* need to move on with our lives... and become a couple." I was sad about this, and a big part of me felt hollow, but there was no sense in torturing ourselves over something that might never be, ever again.

Casey's shoulders drooped, like he was giving up. He repeated into that dark room the very essence of what I'd just said. "If we cannot work things out with Nate over Thanksgiving weekend, then you and I, Zander, will proceed as a couple."

He allowed a deep sigh, which I followed with a deeper one of my own.

THAT'S HOW it's gotta be, bro. And you, you lucky guy, will be in New Hampshire to witness the fallout of our attempt to talk to Nate, whatever it may be. I'm kinda glad about that. I think I'm gonna need you then.

And by the way, did Ma mention to you that, in her usual maternally devoted manner, she's decided to take a late-fall ski vacation at Killington Resort in Vermont for the frigging entire holiday weekend? Yup. No Ma and no "Alex." That's her flavor-of-the-week boyfriend's name. I sure hope Abby can cook.... LOL.

Know what? I'm about 110 percent certain that Casey's family will invite us to Thanksgiving dinner. Mr. and Mrs. Minton are more of a family to me than Ma ever has been. You and Abby will love them.

See you two on Wednesday, early. I've got such mixed emotions about this weekend. Psyched to see you and Abby, worried sick about Casey, freaked out at the prospect of talking to Nate, and worried as hell we won't be able to find him.

But all that has to happen. Time passes and it *will* happen. Didn't know baby bro was so philosophical, did ya?

Later, D.

Z

21
NATE'S DIARY

Sometime right before Thanksgiving, I think—not too fuckin' sure.

CAN'T FUCKIN' believe I even got my frozen-solid fingers to hang on to a pencil. But I got into my truck, and there you were, you dumbass notebook. Sittin' on my fuckin' seat—like the only friend I got left in the world. So I started writin'.

Got my ass fired. Fuck my boss. I wasn't *that* friggin' late for work.

Shit happens. Y'know?

So sick, I am. Not coughin' no more, really. Just feel like crap, head to toe.

Hot, cold, barfy as all hell.

Got no money. Got no gas. Got no beer or pot. Can't even start the goddamn truck no more.

To make matters worse, if that's possible, it's fuckin' freezin' outside.

But I ain't hungry… ain't been hungry in fuckin' days.

Down to one last jug of water that I filled up in the Mickey D's bathroom back when I had gas in my truck.

Then that's all she wrote on the whole "stayin' hydrated" thing too.

Don't give a shit.

And sad to say, this shit ain't the shit that sucks the most in my sorry-ass life.

The worst shit is missin' them two.

Guess I threw 'em away, like Cindy threw me away.

Like everybody and their brother threw me away.

Threw Casey and Zander out before they could throw me out, I did.

Nate DeMarco is a worthless piece of shit.

I ain't even worth the energy it'd take to kill myself.

If I stay here long enough, down by the lake in my frozen-ass truck, no food or drink and sick as a fuckin' dog, I think Mother Nature'll do the job and kill me off.

At least a guy can hope.

Ain't smiled in a long while, but that thought has me grinnin'.

I miss Cindy's whinin'.

Miss my guys.

Miss Casey's soft sweetness.

Miss Zander's I'm-so-cool swagger.

Gonna go to sleep now.

If luck is with me, I won't wake up.

CASEY'S REAL LIFE

DESPITE MY anxiety about what we were planning to do that night, we had a pretty good day on Wednesday. We left Boston City College midmorning and headed straight to Zander's house to spend the day, as his brother Dan and his girlfriend had gotten in late Tuesday night.

We took the train to South Station and then a bus to Concord, where Dan and Abby picked us up at lunchtime.

Zander was so excited to see his older brother that he flung himself into Dan's arms. "Bro, it's so fucking good to see you. Shit, man, I missed your ugly ass."

I supposed this was the way long-lost brothers treated one another. I only had two tiny sisters, and if I said they had ugly asses, my mother would have a word or two to say about it.

"And Abby, my sister, you are looking fine." Zander was in her arms before I could blink. "Abby, this is my boyfriend, Casey. Casey, this is Abby."

"I've heard a lot about you." Abby had warm eyes and a wide smile. She leaned into me and added quietly, "All good things, of course."

I smiled back at her. "Of course."

"So you guys have a kinda big weekend planned, huh?" Dan, who I'd met before and even spent a fair amount of time with over the past few summers, looked at Zander and then at me. "You two up for what you gotta do?"

Well, that was such a direct question. I let Zander reply.

"We have no choice—the two of us are stressing out constantly over this situation with Nate—the time has come to do something about it."

Dan and Abby nodded and looked to me to see if I had something to add. And since they were clearly interested in my opinion, I let my inner chatterbox loose. "I have been having a difficult time with this. I mean, I miss Nate more than you can imagine, but not knowing if we're ever going to connect with him again is killing me. And Zander too. Like, a couple of nights ago, I just couldn't sleep. I kept crying. Zander calmed me down, but... but I can't live like this." My eyes filled and my chest tightened. Before I could stop it, my mouth got dry, and I knew I was going to vomit. "Bathroom...." I left the others to get my duffle bag, and I sprinted into the bus station, searching frantically for a men's room.

It was "a nasty-ass bad scene," as Nate would have said. I vomited repeatedly. My tight chest wouldn't release. But I refused to take the meds that allow me to breathe more easily, because they also put me to sleep. And I couldn't go to sleep, because that evening we were going to deal with Nate.

By the next day, Thanksgiving Day, I would be sitting at my dining room table, eating a traditional turkey dinner, and thanking God for my boyfriends—or my boyfriend.

AFTER A light meal of soup and crackers that Abby decided my fragile stomach could tolerate, I called my parents and told them we were safely back in New Hampshire and that we were going in search of Nate. They knew of our plan to confront him, and although they were anxious for us to reconnect with our third partner, who they loved like a son, they were mainly nervous about me. I had a tendency toward depression, and Mom and Dad wanted to protect me from situations that might upset me.

When I got off the phone, Zander was waiting for me outside in the apartment complex's parking lot, by the passenger seat of his mom's sedan. "What did your parents say?" he asked.

"They just said that they are certain I can handle whatever happens with Nate, you know, that they have confidence in me." I took Zander's hand from the window where it rested and lifted it to my lips for a quick kiss. "But I don't think they hold out much hope for our throuple. In fact, Mom said that when she's driven by the gas station over the past several days, Nate hasn't even been there."

"So she thinks he's moved away or something?"

I tried but couldn't read Zander's expression as he asked me this.

"I don't think they would be shocked if we can't find him tonight." Zander opened the passenger door for me. I climbed in.

Once we were both in the car, Zander spoke again. "Let's start at Missy's house."

"Okay." We had to start somewhere, and that was at the other end of this huge apartment complex, so it made perfect sense.

It only took three minutes to get there. We both hopped out of the car and headed for the stairs. We would walk this difficult road together.

Zander knocked on the front door. And then he knocked again and nobody came to answer.

Nate wasn't in there.

Strike one.

ONCE WE were back in the car, Zander said softly, "Let's try the minimart."

Again I said, "Okay." There was little enthusiasm in my voice.

The minimart was crowded when we got there, as people were getting last minute ingredients and gas for Thanksgiving holiday travel. Nate was not working at the pumps. We didn't even recognize the guy who was attending. So we went into the minimart and were pleased, or at least slightly encouraged, to see Missy behind one of the cash registers.

"Grab a couple bottles of water. We'll get in Missy's line and talk to her while she's ringing them up."

The line moved quickly, and soon we were standing in front of Missy.

"Hi…. Missy, right?"

"Who wants to know?" She didn't look up from the register.

"Um… we're Nate's friends, Zander and Casey." Zander, normally so confident, had a tremor in his voice. "Is he still staying with you?"

At that she looked up, directly into Zander's eyes. "I kicked that asshole out like a week ago."

Zander looked down at me, a flash of concern crossing his brow. "A week ago?"

"Fuck, yeah. He's an asshole." I thought she'd already covered that fact, but for some reason she felt it necessary to repeat.

Finally I opened my mouth. "Where did he go? Where is he living now?"

If looks could kill…. "Ask me if I fucking care."

I felt Zander's hand on the back of my neck. He rubbed a bit, and I tried to relax. "Look, Missy, we need to talk to him. When is he scheduled to work next?"

She grinned, and her already narrow eyes crinkled up at the corners. It was a purely evil grin. "Like… never. Got his nasty ass fired." She fingered her stiff hair, made a halfhearted attempt to flip it over one shoulder, and then snapped her gum.

Zander's hand fell from my neck. We both stared at her.

"When was the last time you saw him?" Zander had a bit more spark left in him than I did.

"Not that I care, but I saw him over at Mickey D's a couple of days ago. He looked like shit, and you can tell him I said so. Now I got customers, so would ya mind clearing out?"

And just like that, we'd been dismissed.

Strike two.

ONCE AGAIN sitting in the car, I looked across the center console. "So what do we do now?"

"I guess we just drive around... you know, look for him," Zander said, staring out over the dashboard.

"We aren't going to be able to find him. You *know* we aren't."

And by mutual agreement, if we didn't find him and deal with this situation, it was over. He was *out* of our relationship. We'd agreed that tonight we'd be a throuple or a couple, but no longer a question mark.

"Well, we're going to give it our very best shot." And Zander started driving.

We checked at McDonald's, and we walked through the Walmart in search of Nate. We hung out at the Starbucks where we'd done our long-ago French project, during which our relationship had been born. We drove around in the back lot behind the grocery store. We circled Benjamin Franklin High School. He was nowhere to be found.

Finally, parked in front of the high school, we admitted our despair.

It sure seemed like strike three.

"What are we going to do, Zander?" I leaned over so my head was on his arm. "What are we going to do?"

And Zander replied, a new confidence ringing in his voice, "We're gonna think like Nate thinks."

And so we brainstormed a list all of the places in town we'd been together, the moments we'd been close and happy, and the places we'd been at those special moments. At basically the exact same instant, it hit us both.

"Down by the lake," we said in unison.

"Nate's in that clearing down by the lake." I restated the now-obvious fact. "In the middle of all the pine trees. I *know* that's where he'd go."

"Yeah. If he's anywhere in this town, it's there. Let's get over there fast."

And just like we thought, when we pulled down the dirt path, we saw that his truck was parked in the little clearing down by the pond.

ZANDER ZANE'S One Voice Blog Spot—by invite only

Your host, Zander Z

I'm writing this story on my blog. No, I'm not ready to share it with anyone but you, Dan. And you were there for a lot of this, man, so you already know much of what I'm gonna write. But I still want to record it, and I figure, what better place to record it than here? I've recently come to the conclusion that it is possible, and maybe very likely, this blog will never be shared with the public. I'm okay with that. This blog is primarily for me. So I can understand. So I can remember.

WHAT ME and Casey found in that truck was devastating. I got to the truck before Casey—like, maybe five big running steps before him. I pulled open the driver's side door, and Nate's big body sort of dropped sideways outta the truck and fell against me. And the most fucked-up part of it was that he never even fucking woke up. My first thought was "He's dead!" But then I saw that he was breathing. So his upper body was dangling out of the truck, and he was sound-the-fuck asleep. Which quickly led me to the new conclusion that he was not just asleep. He was unconscious.

"Zander, what's going on? Why is—" Casey stopped short and gawked at us. "What's wrong with him? Zander, something's wrong with Nate."

Um, yeah. I'd noticed. But I didn't say that to Casey. "Help me get him back into the truck."

Casey immediately ran around to the passenger side. As I gently pushed Nate back in, Casey pulled him from the other side. It took a minute, because Nate was a big dude, but soon we had him flopped down in the other direction, inside the truck.

"He's really cold. Like, *really* cold, Zander." Casey's hands were on Nate's face. "We need to warm him up."

"Let's put him between us."

And that's pretty much what we did. I slid in the driver's side, and we moved Nate so his head was against Casey's chest. I took off my coat and put it on top of him, and then we both cuddled up to him, trying to touch as much of his body as we could to warm him.

After a while, he started to wake up, which was a huge fucking relief. First he struggled to get free of us, almost automatically. But when he finally opened his eyes and focused on me, then on Casey, and then on me again, he said plainly, "I'm dead."

That was a pretty alarming statement. Casey and I exchanged wary glances. But since he clearly wasn't dead, we both shrugged and focused our attention back on him.

On this newest version of Nate, that is. This guy was not the Nate we knew. In fact, he wasn't even the burnout Nate we knew from freshman year in high school. He wasn't the pissed-off Nate we'd met who'd broken up with us either. This Nate was a shell of the most broken and despondent version of Nate DeMarco that I could imagine.

So I was sure he wasn't dead, at that point. His eyes were open and blinking, and he was moving around. But he sure did look like hell. His skin was gray, his hair was one ginormous knot, and his mouth and lips were dry and cracking. I remembered an experiment I learned one summer in camp, and I pinched the back of Nate's icy cold hand. The skin was slow to go back into place. I recalled that this was a bad sign.

"I think he's superdehydrated. I'm gonna run up to the car and get those bottles of water," I said to Casey, reaching for the door.

"You don't need to. I have mine in my coat pocket." Casey leaned forward and pulled his water bottle out of his coat, unscrewed the cap, and held it to Nate's lips. At first, Nate shook his head and refused it. I thought maybe he was still dazed and confused. But then his better judgment, or maybe it was instinct, inspired him to drink. He drank like a baby from a bottle, with Casey holding it to his lips.

After he drank a good portion of the water, he started to shiver, and I thought maybe he was coming back to life. I said, "Hey, man, think you can walk? You need to get into my car, and we can put the heat on really high."

Nate nodded dully. He still wasn't fully with the program. With great effort, we slid out of the truck, inching out the passenger door. With Nate between us, one arm resting over each of our shoulders, we stumbled all the way up to the car. When we got there, Nate bent over, like right in half, and barfed out a good portion of the water he'd just sucked down. He was in worse shape than I'd thought.

Once we got him seated in the passenger side of the car, still staring blankly like he didn't know up from down, I cranked the heat. When the warmth hit his face, he closed his eyes and basked in it like a cat on a sunny windowsill.

"We should take him to the hospital, shouldn't we?" Casey asked from the backseat.

"Probably. I think he's dehydrated and kinda frozen."

And that's when Nate made his second statement—the first since "I'm dead."

"Don't wanna."

So I asked the obvious. "What *do* you want?"

Casey leaned forward to hear his answer.

But instead of answering, Nate just sort of melted down. He slumped forward in the seat and then made a howling sort of sound that didn't stop for what seemed like a very long time.

Danny, my heart frigging broke for Nate right then. I could see and hear the signs—he was completely fucking broken. And then, as soon as my heart put itself back together, the surge of love that came forth from it could have knocked over a brick wall.

"We'll do whatever you want."

I knew, bro, right then, that I'd wait forever for this guy. I love him that much.

"I love you, Nate." The nearly inaudible words came from the backseat, along with a small hand that snaked its way around Nate's chest. "I love you, Nate." Apparently Casey was experiencing the very same overwhelming feelings of love for Nate that I was. "Take him to your mom's apartment. We can take care of him there."

And just before I put the car in drive, Nate did the strangest thing I'd ever seen him do. Right there in the front seat, he turned on his side and tried to curl up into a fetal ball. His long legs folded up beneath him, his back curved in around his middle, and he wrapped both arms around his body, as if to comfort himself.

Casey and I exchanged yet another "holy shit" glance, and then I drove like a bat outta hell toward our place. I mean, can you blame me?

BY THE time we got back to the apartment, Nate had fallen asleep again. He was sitting beside me all whitish-gray, with dry red lips, curled up as much as a big guy in the front seat of a sedan could get. And his head kept falling backward. That he looked like the living dead, as in a vampire, crossed my mind more than a few times. His cheekbones were protruding, as was his collarbone. I could see the top part of his chest above his collar. He'd definitely dropped a lot of pounds since we'd been together.

We woke him gently, but he still startled like a nervous cat. His eyes got wide and stayed that way. From this point, Dan, you were around to witness the ugliness, but still I want to make a record of it.

Casey and I had to drag him outta the truck. He didn't want to move. The thing that struck me hardest, though, was that he didn't seem to recognize Casey and me. When I looked into his eyes, Nate DeMarco wasn't looking back, you know? There was nobody home. It's hard to describe, but it was super fucked up.

Once we got him inside, you and Abby were there to help us. The first thing we did was get him settled on the couch. That's when I noticed he wasn't wearing a T-shirt under his button down, and by the looks of it, he didn't have any boxers on under his jeans. No coat either. It was like he was sitting in his truck, with no heat on, dressed for summer, just waiting to freeze to death.

I knew Nate had given up. On everything. On Cindy, on us… on life.

My head throbbed and felt tight, like it was gonna burst from emotional overload. Why hadn't he come to us, told us he was down and out to this extent, and asked for help?

"Hey, sweetheart. Looks like you've had a rough time of it." Casey was sitting beside Nate on the couch, rubbing his knee. "You okay with this? With being here on Zander's couch and out of the cold?"

Casey was asking permission to proceed with lifesaving measures from a virtual zombie. Nate turned to him and stared into Casey's eyes. It was as if he were trying to remember who Casey was, what he had meant to him. But he nodded.

Abby came to us right then with a big, puffy, unzipped sleeping bag in her arms and placed it over Casey and Nate. Then, Dan, you said, "Zander, why don't you sit down on Nate's other side? Comfort him and warm him up."

I was having my own zombie moment. I remember staring at you, trying to make sense of your words. I guess the intensity of the situation had overwhelmed me. But I slipped beneath the sleeping bag beside Nate and reached one arm around his shoulders. I swear he leaned toward me a few inches.

"Dude, you hungry? Thirsty?"

Nate turned to me and stared like he'd stared at Casey a minute before. He nodded. "Thirsty. Nothin' to drink since yesterday, 'cept for what I…."

Except for what he barfed on the ground, down by the river.

"I'll go get him some water." Abby left the room.

"Nate, I think we should take you over to the emergency room and get you checked out." Casey again seemed to be asking for permission to administer medical care.

But Nate wasn't giving it. "No." Short and sweet. He didn't want to go. "Can I... can I just sit here... awhile?"

I blurted out an answer before any of us had a chance to think. "You can sit here, buddy, for as long as you want."

Again Nate nodded and refocused his eyes on the nothingness before him.

Abby brought a glass of water and a bowl of chicken noodle soup and crackers left over from dinner. She put them on the coffee table in front of him, and he studied the bowl of soup as if he'd never come across one before. "Can I eat it?" He looked at Abby for permission. Her eyes flooded with tears before she nodded.

What the fuck had happened to him? It had been barely six weeks since we'd had him in our bed down at BCC and he was making love to us with tenderness. And now he hardly knew who we were? He was barely even a shell of the guy we spent almost two years with.

Right then, without a shadow of a doubt, I knew I needed to change that. He was ours. Nate DeMarco belonged to Casey and me. And we belonged to him.

We needed each other to be whole. The evidence was right there in front of me, drooling over a bowl of Campbell's Chicken Noodle Soup.

I lifted the bowl of soup and held it by his chest. Casey handed Nate the spoon. "Eat, Nate."

Nate cautiously took the spoon from Casey's hand. You and Abby went back into the kitchen at that point. You guys knew he wouldn't want to be stared at while he ate. And after he took one bite, it was like he couldn't resist. He started wolfing down the soup like he hadn't eaten in days. And it hit me—he probably *hadn't* eaten in days.

"Crackers... uh... please."

I noticed that Nate's dark eyes were fixed on the plate of saltines.

"Ain't eaten for like... like two days or so, and I'm...."

Casey lifted the plate and offered them to him. Nate was clearly too hungry to hold back, like the soup had awakened his taste buds.

"Want me to go make you a sandwich, Nate?"

Casey always tried to feed us, so it didn't surprise me. Casey started to stand up, but Nate grasped Casey's hand in his fist. He made a sound that resembled the word "no," so Casey sat back down.

"I'll stay here, sweetie. I won't go anywhere."

Again Casey and I looked at each other. We tried not to show that we were floored by Nate's desperation. After Nate finished eating, he gulped down the entire glass of water and leaned back on the couch.

"Would it be all right if I took your temperature? Your skin feels warm."

Casey was pressing on with his caretaking efforts. Again, Nate refused.

He shook his head. "Can I take a shower?"

"Of course you can." I didn't attempt to jump up and grab him a towel, though. I was gonna let Nate make the first move.

After a full two minutes, while Casey and I studied him and he studied the air in front of his face, he finally made the effort to stand up. We did the same, and I headed for the stairs. Nate and Casey trailed behind me to the bathroom near my bedroom.

I didn't want to let Nate out of my sight for as much as a minute. So I led him into the bathroom, and I just didn't leave. Casey didn't turn to head out the door either. I turned on the shower, felt the water a few times with my hand to set it at the perfect temperature, and grabbed a clean towel off the shelf. Then I stood there. Right beside Casey. We watched as Nate began to unbutton.

His fingers weren't working very well, probably too frozen for too long to have their full coordination back. So Casey stepped forward and asked, "May I help you?"

Dropping his hands to his sides, Nate nodded and uttered a muffled, "Thanks."

I watched as Casey slowly undressed Nate, first unbuttoning and removing his shirt, revealing a bony chest, and then moving to his pants. As I'd suspected, Nate wore no underwear, so when Casey slid his pants down and pulled them off, along with his unlaced boots, he was completely naked. He made no attempt to cover himself. As soon as he was naked, he just stepped into the shower.

Casey nudged me and whispered, "What's up with Nate? He's so *different*."

I shrugged.

"Are we back together now?" Casey looked so hopeful.

But I shrugged again. I had no idea what we were. "Let's just take things moment by moment, 'kay?" I reached my arm around Casey and pulled him against me, knowing he needed it. We stood like statues until Nate turned the water off. I offered him a towel before he had to ask for one. He stood inside the shower for a few minutes, toweling off, before he stepped out with the towel wrapped around his waist.

Nate didn't seem embarrassed or uncomfortable and not nearly as awkward as me and Casey. Finally he asked, "Can we go to bed?"

Casey voiced my question. "We?"

"Uh-huh." It was that simple. "Got an extra toothbrush I can use?"

After I found Nate a new toothbrush in the back of the linen closet, we all took turns in the bathroom, answering nature's call, brushing our teeth and stuff. Then we were off to my bedroom. I pushed back the bedspread, and Nate tried to scoot up against the wall. I grabbed him by the arm and stopped him in the middle of my double bed. Casey sort of automatically knew what to do. We were like some kind of a loving-Nate tag team. He climbed right over Nate, and I got in on the edge of the bed. We put Nate in the middle. We wanted him between us, where we could both touch him and hold him and let him know we were there for him. Okay, okay—so *we* could know he was really there with us.

Nate lay flat on his back staring at the ceiling, totally detached. I had about a million questions for him, and knowing Casey, he probably had two million questions. But this was enough for now.

I was glad that, at this point, Casey took charge. He pulled Nate onto his side and threw his arms around his neck, pressing his face to Nate's chest. I watched to see if Nate would reach around to hold Casey too, but he didn't.

I didn't let that hold me back from wrapping one arm around his shoulder and the other around his hip. I also didn't let the feeling of his newly protruding hipbone, which was poking uncomfortably into my arm, prevent me from embracing him. Casey and I continued to act as the tag team, clearly on the same page. We rubbed his chest, his shoulders, and his arms. We snuggled against him, placing our still-clothed bodies against his bare skin, our faces against his chest and back.

But neither of us kissed him. We were there as his friends, not his lovers. We were there to support him, not seduce him.

After about an hour of clasping Nate to our hearts, he started to cry. I don't know how I knew he was crying. His chest wasn't racked with sobs. He made no noise. I just knew. And I was sure that Casey knew too.

An occasional sniff, a muffled whimper, a couple of staggered breaths. Those were the only clues we had.

"We love you, Nate." Casey's sweet voice rang out in the darkness. "Just know that we still love you."

Nate froze, as if he were waiting for something.

So I delivered. "We never forgot about you for a second. We missed you and we waited for you and... we're still waiting."

That was when Nate let loose with the sobs. I'd never seen someone cry so desperately. Like he was brokenhearted. Or maybe just broken.

He began to speak between the thick sound of sobs. "Cindy... and Uncle Rich... I don't deserve love... gonna fuck it up with you too... all alone... *should* be alone... loser... no job... no life... thought I died... was glad of it too."

It had all caught up with him. Nate's life of fear, pain, and tragedy had caught up to him at that very moment, as we held him between us.

"You are a precious gem to us, Nate." Casey's voice was sweet and sincere. "It doesn't matter how anyone else—or how the world at large—sees you, sweetheart. You are a precious gem in our eyes."

At hearing those perfect words, I cried too. I couldn't help it.

"Can... can I...." He tried, but he couldn't spit out his question.

"Can you what, Nate?" Casey was holding himself together, and for that I was thankful.

"C-can I c-come back to you guys?"

That's when Casey let himself cry too.

The three of us, smashed together on the very center of my double bed like too many kittens in a too-small basket, bawled like babies.

"Yeah, man. Yeah, we want you back." I choked out my consent.

"You were always ours, Nate. You were *always* part of us," Casey said, sounding more composed than either me or Nate.

"I missed ya so bad... fuckin' missed bein' us three... wanna be back...."

"You never left, dude. Our hearts... in our hearts you never left." I said it twice, in different ways, so there was no way he could miss it.

It took a good long while, but in time we got on the same page.

"I love you—my best friends, and brothers, and lovers."

"I'm never gonna stop loving you dudes either."

"Lovin' ya... lovin' ya so fuckin' much...." Nate was the last of us three to declare his love.

It was like we were once again singing the same song in one strong voice.

CASEY'S REAL LIFE

THANKSGIVING WAS nothing like I pictured it. We didn't dress up and head to my house to celebrate the things and people we were thankful for in the company of my sweet-natured mother, my slightly nerdy father, and my two adorable little sisters in their matching velvet dresses. Dad didn't make a big show of carving the turkey, and Mom didn't wear her "Kiss the Cook" apron. Lola and Sarah didn't spend the afternoon tracing their fingers and then coloring in their handprint turkey pictures. We didn't share laughs about days gone by over homemade pumpkin pie.

This Thanksgiving was different. But I was more profoundly thankful than I had ever been before.

The three of us were together again, which was all that mattered.

And we were all hurt and damaged, still suffering from the time we'd spent apart. Zander and I struggled to trust. Nate struggled to so much as breathe, let alone communicate what had happened to him while we had been apart. Our beautiful throuple was dented and scratched and stood on three shaky legs. But it stood again, and that was the important fact.

We woke up gradually. None of us was willing to be the first to open our eyes and discover that Nate's return to us was just a wishful dream. Nate was the last to open his eyes. He knew, I'm sure, that we would want to talk, and Nate was not one to easily spill the contents of his heart and mind.

"Happy Thanksgiving, you guys." That was how I said good morning, which I did the split second Nate's right eye sleepily blinked open. "Let's go downstairs and eat breakfast. I can make us omelets." I figured the best way to start a difficult day, like today was certain to be, would be with full stomachs. Nate nodded. I heard his stomach growl loudly. Yes, he needed to eat.

"Abby and Dan told me they went grocery shopping yesterday morning. We should have all the ingredients for an awesome omelet and probably home fries too," Zander said with a matter-of-fact attitude that I was certain he wasn't feeling.

Zander and I had both chosen to ignore the elephant in the room.

Nate was still subdued. He nodded and said, "Gotta use the can."

Zander slid off the bed so Nate could go to the bathroom. I'm sure we both fought the urge to follow him. We were paranoid that he'd jump out the window and be lost to us again.

After we all cleaned up, we traipsed down to the kitchen, where Abby and Dan were already drinking coffee.

So yes, it was a bit awkward.

"Morning, dudes." Dan's language was similar to Zander's. "You three sleep okay?"

Standing in a straight line across the wide entrance to the kitchen, we nodded in unison.

"Care for some coffee?" Abby didn't wait for answers. She went to the cupboard to get mugs and started pouring.

"I'll make myself tea." I headed to the stove.

Silence.

"Your father stopped by, Casey."

I turned to look at Dan.

"While you guys were still sleeping. He said they would bring us a turkey dinner later, so we shouldn't worry about going anywhere or fixing a meal."

Abby added, "They're very cool."

"Yeah, they are," Zander agreed. Nate just stared from Abby to Dan.

"So anyway, Abby and I were thinking of going for a run, and… I think we're gonna head out, like, right now. So we'll see you guys later. Okay?"

I could tell they were clearing out for our benefit, and I felt bad. This was Abby's first visit to her boyfriend's house. So far his mother had left for the entire weekend, and she was basically being kicked out of the kitchen.

Nate blushed, so I knew he was aware of what was happening around him.

"I'm making omelets. I'll have them waiting for you on the counter for when you get back from your run."

"Thanks for the offer, Casey, but we ate hours ago. You guys take all the time you need, and we'll catch you later." Dan and Abby stepped out of the kitchen, leaving the three of us alone again.

Nate dropped into a kitchen chair and sipped on the coffee Abby had poured. He hadn't made eye contact with us yet that morning and was still avoiding it by gazing into his coffee. I turned back to the stove as Zander brought me the eggs, milk, ham, cheese, and potatoes for home fries.

"I fucked up real bad." Surprisingly, Nate spoke first. "Don't know how to say sorry for it."

I heard the sound of a chair being dragged out and a short sigh as Zander sat down. "We need to talk it out, dude. We need to figure out how things went to hell in a fucking handbasket."

"I just fucked up, 'kay?" Nate sounded impatient, as if he wanted the conversation to be over. It hadn't even started.

"No. It's not 'okay.'" Zander's voice was equally tense. "We are gonna talk, dude."

I poured the egg mixture into the waiting pan. Then I started chopping the potatoes and just listened.

"You guys know what set me off. I screwed up royally with Cindy."

"You need to tell us what happened there, Nate. We never got the full story," Zander suggested.

By the way Nate sighed, I could tell he was still agitated. "My asshole uncle choked her... near to death."

That was a rather simplistic explanation for the incident that set off this painful chain of events.

"Did you go straight to the hospital from BCC, you know, that day you took off?"

Nate nodded. "Do I really have to go over this shit with you? It sucked when it was goin' down, and it sucks every time I think about it."

I dropped slices of ham and cheese on top of the eggs, but I still didn't say anything.

"Nate, you *left* us. You fucking took off and left us. You never explained shit to us. You never even fucking broke up with us. We had to come and find you so you could dump us on our asses."

I swallowed hard and closed up the omelet with the rubber spatula. It seemed that Nate had nothing to say.

"You've gotta open up to us, dude." I glanced behind me and saw that Zander was walking around the table. "We frigging *love* you, man. We *need* you. We aren't complete without you. Shit. You got hurt, and I can see that and it sucks. But you hurt *us* too."

"I can't fuckin' *do* this." Nate, wearing nothing but one of Zander's loosest T-shirts, a borrowed pair of boxers, and his dirty jeans from the day before—not even wearing shoes—jumped out of the chair and headed across the kitchen toward the front door, like he was leaving. "I'm so fuckin' outta here."

I slid the pan off the burner but refused to turn around and watch him walk out on us again. It would kill me to see him go one more time, and I knew that if he left us now, it was over. Not only for our throuple but for Nate himself. He seemed to have a death wish.

"No. You aren't walking out on us again, asshole." Zander had jumped up as well. "Fight for us, DeMarco, like we're fighting for you."

Then there was a tense stillness. It was too quiet, and I waited, not daring to so much as breathe.

"I'm a goddamn fuckin' screw-up. I screwed up with Cindy. I screwed up what us three had goin'. I ain't good for you guys to be with." His voice broke on his last word.

I finally turned around. "Do you love us?" It was a simple question. And if his answer was in the affirmative, it was the only thing that mattered. We could figure things out from there.

Nate staggered like he'd been shot and dropped to his knees. Zander and I gawked at him. He crumbled to the floor and curled into a ball. "You guys shoulda let me die out there." His words were muffled yet audible.

We both pounced on him. When we were all piled together on the kitchen floor, I couldn't stop myself—I grabbed his cheek in one hand rather roughly and asked again, "Do you love us? Answer me."

He nodded, but that wasn't enough.

"Answer in *words*. Do you love us and want to be with us?" I think I shook his face, and harshly too. "*Do you?*" I was crying again, but that wasn't surprising.

Nate pushed himself up so he was sitting cross-legged, and he looked right into my teary eyes with his own serious dark ones. "Casey, *of course* I love you guys. How the fuck could I *not* love you?" He glanced at Zander.

"Then promise you won't walk out the door on us again." Zander put words to my thoughts. "We need to know that you're here with us in this. In the good times as well as in the shitty ones."

The sight of my two partners, the torment in their still-dry eyes, felt like knives piercing my gut. I could do nothing but wait for Nate to pronounce a life or death sentence on our relationship.

"I don't wanna go. I love you guys. And if I left, I'd leave to... I'd leave so that I could just pass on from here."

I was certain that by "here" he meant from the world. He was prepared to go away to die.

"Cuz sometimes... sometimes shit just hurts too fuckin' much...."

I could sense that Nate was about to open his heart to us. The anticipation made me shiver.

"And when I knew I screwed up so bad with Cindy, I felt like shit. I let her get nearly killed, and I knew I didn't deserve to feel none of the warm lovin' feelin's you guys gave me no more. Didn't deserve it, cuz I proved myself to be a selfish asshole. I stayed with you two that night cuz *I wanted to*. Not cuz *you* wanted me to, Zander, though I blamed it on your ass. I friggin' didn't wanna go home, where I felt so empty and got beat on all the fuckin' time, and... it was just so nice there with you guys."

I had so much to say, but I held back. Nate was releasing his feelings, and I needed to listen.

"I got to the hospital, and they treated me like a fuckin' stranger. Somehow they'd already got a hold of Aunt Terri, and she sorta got put in charge. When Cin... when Cindy came to, she told Terri that she fuckin' hated me for leavin' her at home alone with Uncle Rich. Said she was gonna fuckin' hate me forever. She still ain't talked to me to this day."

Zander moved behind Nate so he could lean back against him. I bent forward and grasped his hands in mine and then squeezed to encourage him to keep talking.

"I figured, in time, you guys were gonna dump my sorry ass too. You guys—friggin' college guys now—were gonna smarten up to who the fuck ya let in ya bed. And I'll tell ya this. It'd be easier to go to sleep alone in that parkin' lot and never wake up than it'd be to have you guys turn on me. And hate me… like Cindy does."

"That won't ever happen. We love you. We weren't able to smile at all since you left us. We felt empty and lonely. We missed you more than you can imagine." I squeezed his hands as I spoke. "But we need to know if you're back for good."

This time he didn't hesitate. "I wanna be. Only thing is, I'm a big screw-up."

That's when Zander laughed. It came from down low in his chest. "Yeah, dude, but you're *our* screw-up, and we wanna keep you."

Nate smiled at that. And then he told us how he'd lost his home, his job, his health, and finally, he thought, maybe even his sanity. What a picture the three of us must have made, sitting on Zander's kitchen floor, huddled together for shelter, safety, and comfort.

When he had finished his story, including the details of his uncle's arrest and Cindy's relocation to Aunt Terri's house, I decided it was time to make things more upbeat. "I'm fairly certain I can salvage the omelets, but I'm thinking no home fries at this point. Zander, will you put in some toast and butter it? And Nate, how about pouring three tall glasses of OJ?"

The three of us made breakfast, ate breakfast, and cleaned up from breakfast as if six weeks of pain hadn't recently separated us.

ZANDER ZANE'S One Voice Blog Spot—by invite only

Your host, Zander Z

More for the record book. Just saying. Marking this entry as for my eyes only.

****Note to self*—this part is not for Dan's eyes or for a One Voice blog entry or for anyone but me.

After breakfast, right about when Dan and Abby got back from their run, Casey and I took Nate back to the bedroom. We had a fairly clear idea of what Nate had endured. We knew he was devastated by the loss of his little sister and he was afraid of losing us in the same kinda way. He had no job, no money, and he was homeless. We also knew that he still loved us and wanted to be with us.

This time when we placed Nate between us in the bed, he didn't act dazed and unaware of us. This time he showed us his neediness. And seeing him needy for us was the biggest boost we could ever have hoped for. Before we got into my bed, we all stripped down to our underwear. We wanted to press as much of our skin together as possible. I think that might be what I missed most about being a throuple—lying together, feeling each other's bodies, languishing in the sense of warmth, safety, and belonging. Not to be overly dramatic or anything.

And so we did just that for three hours. Dan and Abby probably wondered if the earth had opened up and swallowed us.

Nate was acting a lot more like Casey than I'd ever seen before. He kept flipping back and forth between us, reaching out to pull Casey against him, kissing him lightly on the forehead, and then turning toward me to do the same. The dude flipped back and forth so many times that he was getting me dizzy. So, finally I gently pushed him onto his back and leaned down to kiss him soundly. Casey, realizing that I was trying to get Nate's mind focused, leaned over and started to kiss his neck and throat. When we had his complete attention, both of us pulled ourselves up beside him and studied his face.

"You are beautiful," Casey told him.

Nate shook his head.

"You are ours," I informed him.

Nate nodded.

"Is it okay if we make love to you? I mean, I think I'm speaking for both of us when I say that we want to have our fill of you, and the only way we can do that is to take you to heaven with our bodies and—"

I could tell Casey was back to his normal self, as he was chattering happily. Even Nate smiled.

"Can we love you, dude? You ready for that?" I interrupted Casey to simplify the question.

"I… uh… I'm all skinny, and I ain't shaved in a month and…."

"That sounds like a yes to me," I said and winked at Casey, who winked back.

"Okay." Nate released a long breath. Then he added, "Yeah, please… please, you guys. Love on my body."

We didn't need to hear another word on the subject. Not another fucking word.

Casey and I started our work, but before we did, I hesitated a second to take in the moment. I looked at Nate lying beneath me. He was skinny as a rail but as lanky and beautiful as ever, arms and legs splayed beside him, eyes wide and expectant, and barely breathing as he waited for us to deliver him to paradise. And Casey, whose light eyes were locked on Nate's lips, probably in anticipation of what he was gonna do to them, was smiling. Clearly *he* was already in heaven.

"I love you guys." They both turned their heads to look at me when I said that. And in their eyes, I saw everything I would ever need.

Casey went to work on Nate's lips, and Nate's eyes rolled back before closing. These two dudes meant everything to me, and I swore to myself that I would never again let anything divide us. Then I bent down to Nate's bony chest and tasted his skin.

I needed to reacquaint myself with every inch of his body, so I started with his left nipple, which was as good a starting point as any. I took it between my lips. Nate shuddered and would have gasped if Casey hadn't been attached to his mouth by the lips. I put that nipple through a lot, sucking it and biting on it and giving it like a thousand tiny kisses. I had to know if my efforts were successful, so I reached down and stuck my hand on the crotch of Nate's boxers. I couldn't miss that his dick was begging for attention.

But it wasn't time to take care of that yet. I gave his dick a little pat and then climbed between his legs so I could pay some attention to his belly. Every inch of this guy needed loving attention.

And between Casey and me, every inch was gonna get it. Before I got down to business, I glanced at Nate's upper body and saw that Casey had moved down from his lips and was licking Nate's jaw and the hollow of his neck. I couldn't see Nate's face anymore, but I'd seen his expression in moments like this, and it was always one of complete surrender. And it was always a fucking beautiful sight. With that image in my mind, I lowered my face to his belly and pressed my cheek against the fur there. It was the best feeling in the world.

By the time Casey and I had finished kissing Nate all over—I'd had a field day on his hips, legs, and feet, and Casey had taken care of his arms and hands and chest—Nate lay flat on the bed, gripping the bedspread and breathing heavily, like he was trying hard to stay in control. His eyes were closed tightly. He appeared completely helpless, and I liked it.

I wanted complete submission from Nate. From the devilish expression on Casey's face as he feasted those baby blues on Nate's crotch, he did too.

"Open your eyes, Nate. Look at us." I was surprised by the commanding sound of my voice.

He quickly complied. In the depths of his eyes, I saw the true fragility of this normally strong man. I saw surrender. And I knew he was ours.

Together Casey and I removed his boxers and began feeding on his dick as if we'd been starving for him—because we had been.

My eager lips and tongue met with Casey's as we took him into our mouths. It was also the closest I had felt to Casey in months. Nate struggled not to buck his hips, thrusting his dick into whichever mouth was open to it. By staying still, he was submitting to our will, which was what we all needed. The ache of separation, though still echoing in my head, was no longer true pain. It was in the past, and we were reestablishing our connection. It may have seemed like we were simply reconnecting our bodies, but the moment went way far beyond that. It was about our hearts.

I had to jump up for a second to retrieve the lube I'd stuffed in my backpack in a hopeful moment before we left BCC. By the time I returned, Casey was already coaching Nate to get on all fours. He obediently crouched on the center of the bed, and Casey slid directly underneath him. I prepared Nate for sex carefully but quickly. None of us were in a position to wait very long for the next chapter of our lovemaking.

Pushing inside of Nate right then was not an experience I'll ever forget. The moment is a permanent part of my memory now. Engraved on my brain, you know? And his body didn't want to just let me right in. He had to struggle to accept me, which paralleled the struggle of his heart. It wasn't easy for Nate to open his body or his heart to us, but with a bit of persistence, he allowed both.

I moved inside him, at first slowly and deeply, touching his inner depths. It made him gasp over and over, which sounded better than any music. When my movements became shallower, more satisfying to my own needs, I heard the muffled sound of moaning coming from beneath me in stereo, and I knew Casey was also very busy, probably stroking himself and Nate in time with my thrusts.

"Kiss Casey, Nate. Kiss him right now," I demanded, just when I knew I was ready to come. I wanted their lips joined at my moment of completion. Nate immediately lowered himself to his elbows and then turned his head slightly to the side so he could cover Casey's lips with his own. Seeing that, I lost all control and released everything I had—everything I'd held inside for so long— right into Nate's body. And in my mind, through Nate's lips, my love flowed into Casey as well. Before another second had passed, Nate was stiffening beneath me in the manner of a man letting go. Then Casey reached up, and his hand covered mine on Nate's hip. When he squeezed, I knew he was coming too.

I was the first to say it. "I love you guys. We're never gonna be apart again."

Casey's words of love were breathless as well. "I love my guys… love you two."

But Nate's words cut through what little was left of the residual darkness and fogginess that kept us from complete intimacy. Nate said, "I'm alive."

****NOTE TO *self:* okay to post this part

So Dan—

That night the Mintons came over. They brought a holiday with them. Casey, Nate, and I, along with Abby, you, and the twins, chowed down on the best turkey dinner we've ever eaten. Which isn't really saying much, because you know better than anybody that Ma's cooking kinda sucks.

After we ate, we popped in the video of *Frozen* to entertain Sarah and Lola, who looked supercute in matching velvety dark green dresses with big shiny bows on their backs. The rest of us sat in the living room drinking coffee and tea, eating pumpkin pie, and talking quietly. I felt like we had a real family, not just you, me, Ma, her latest fuck buddy, and maybe a stray uncle—which was our normal holiday, growing up.

Didn't you like how Mr. and Mrs. Minton talked to Nate about his future options? They weren't in his face about it at all. They were cool and concerned—and just right.

I loved it when Mr. Minton said to Casey, Nate, and me, "You three boys are *all* our sons. We love you all, and we want to see each one of you happily working on your future goals. That means you too, Nate."

Nate definitely had a "what the fuck?" moment when Mr. Minton said that. His jaw dropped about three inches, remember?

Mrs. Minton said, "Nate, one of my former college roommates works in admissions at the Boston Culinary Institute near Boston City College. If you want, I'll put in a call and see what's necessary to get you in there, starting second semester. And she can help me figure out financial aid for you, as well."

Nate got a worried look on his face, which made Casey practically jump into his lap.

Remember when Nate said, "I ain't got nowhere to live"?

When you and Abby went into the kitchen for coffee, Mr. Minton told us not to worry. He explained that, since Casey's on a full scholarship, the Mintons would be willing to pay for an apartment for us with the cash they'd saved for Casey's college education.

That family is more a family to me than Ma *ever* was—and definitely more of a family to Nate than his own mom and uncle. Get this, dude—later that night, Casey's parents told Nate that he could stay in Casey's room at their house until we found an apartment for all three of us. That was really cool of them to offer, but we aren't gonna take them up on it. Nate belongs with the two of us, and we plan to smuggle him into our dorm room and keep him with us until we have an apartment.

Eventful Turkey Day weekend, right? Glad you and Abby were there to share the drama. Abby's a keeper. Just saying.

Shit, did you get the we-are-family vibe when we all ate Thanksgiving dinner together at our place? You and Abby included. And then when we went over to the Mintons' house for games and leftovers on Saturday? Wasn't it like we fucking belonged?

There I go getting all sappy again, but I will admit, I was into it.

Tomorrow, back to classes for all of us. But your baby bro isn't all torn apart in the head and heart anymore. And for the record, I know Nate didn't talk too much this weekend, but first of all, he never is much of a chatterbox—that's Casey's job—and second, he's still getting over his ordeal, plus I think he was missing his little sister, Cindy, something fierce.

We're gonna work on that situation once Nate is on his feet again.

Fucking loved seeing you guys.

Talk soon.

Zander

CASEY'S REAL LIFE

DEEP EMOTIONAL trauma changes a person. Over Thanksgiving weekend, after we made love and recommitted ourselves to one another, I noticed that Nate was slightly more remote than he was before our breakup. He was also very cautious with every word he said. I would swear he thought and rethought every sentence he uttered to Zander and me.

But I understood. Seeing Nate behave with such detachment brought me back to the most emotionally difficult days in my own life. It dragged me back to the severe beating I took from Liz Trainer during junior year of high school. It had taken me weeks and weeks, if not months, to let go of the emotional strain from that ordeal and to fully rejoin the world. Nate is definitely the strong, silent type by nature, but I still had to remind myself that it would take some time for this remote and distressed version of Nate to find the more secure Mr. Strong and Silent again.

We spent most of the weekend at Zander's house, where we normally would have spent it at mine. Nate needed time to readjust to our relationship, and we felt that he would do that best by being alone with us. Up in Zander's room, we spent the better part of our time lying together on the bed, the three of us in a tight row, Nate always curled up in the middle, while Zander and I watched mindless television or studied. Nate didn't seem to want a diversion other than our presence. He often kept his eyes closed, but he was always touching us as much as possible.

Hands splayed on our thighs, feet hooked around our ankles, face pressed to our sides—Nate needed physical connection. And so did we.

It was striking to see such an imposing, potentially dominant man behave like a frightened child, curled docilely between Zander and me. But it was beautiful that he trusted us enough to let his guard down.

On Sunday, when it was time to return to school, Nate became agitated, like a child would before a dreaded doctor's visit.

Zander wanted to spend time with his brother and his girlfriend before we all left to go back to our respective colleges, so we ventured downstairs earlier than we had on previous days. Nate was still dressed in all of Zander's clothes—his T-shirt, boxers, and sweatpants—even though Zander and Dan had retrieved the two big plastic trash bags from the bed of Nate's truck, inside of which were all of his earthly belongings. I had washed and folded every item of Nate's clothing, and Zander had filled a box with Nate's other personal items. They all sat in the corner of his bedroom. Nonetheless, Nate seemed perfectly comfortable to be outfitted in Zander's clothing. With his weight loss, the clothes more or less fit. I thought it made him feel further connected to one of his boyfriends to be dressed in Zander's clothes.

"Good morning, Abby. Morning, Dan," I greeted them as I entered the kitchen. "I'm thinking of making chocolate chip pancakes this morning. We need to fatten up this guy." I patted Nate's rear end, and he blushed. "Anybody up for pancakes?"

They all raised their hands slyly.

"Well, then, I'll get right to it."

"There's coffee." Abby spoke sweetly but kind of tentatively. "How do you take yours, Nate?"

Nate leaned against the doorway. "You don't have to fix it for me, Abby. I can do it."

Abby stood up from her chair and went right to Nate. Again, he turned red. "I want to fix your coffee for you, Nate. Let a houseguest make herself feel useful, okay?"

"Well, sure. Uh, thanks, ma'am."

"Ma'am?" Abby looked like she was ready to jump out of her skin, but instead she impulsively grabbed Nate by the shoulders. "Never call me *ma'am*. That's for housewives and spinster librarians, and I am neither. It's Abby, Abster, Ab, or sis, but never ma'am." She turned toward the counter to pour Nate's coffee.

"I take it black." Nate smiled. "Just plain, like me."

"You gonna fix *my* coffee, Abster?" I could tell that Zander was just loving the playful interaction with this woman who might one day be his sister.

"You, on the other hand, Zander, can call me ma'am." Delivering that zinger, she never even turned to look at Zander.

The ice was broken, I made pancakes, and we talked like a family.

"I start my guidance prepracticum in January. I'm really looking forward to it. I'm doing it in a high school about twenty minutes from Northwestern. Three other students are also student teaching there, and one has a car. If I pitch in for gas, I can ride along." Dan was practically glowing with excitement at his first taste of the classroom.

"Can't wait 'til that's me, dude. But I got a load more classes to take before they'll let me near the kids," Zander said.

Dan shifted his attention to me. "And you're premed, Casey?"

"Yeah. Bio and statistics major."

Everybody groaned.

"What sort of doctor do you want to be?" Abby appeared genuinely interested.

"Not sure yet. I have time to figure that out." I wanted to bring Nate into the conversation. "And my mom is going to look into the cooking school, Boston Culinary Institute, for Nate to attend starting second semester."

"You should've let Nate make the pancakes."

Dan was joking, but I knew Nate would be embarrassed.

But Zander stepped in to save the day. "Not so much. He's not a chef *yet*."

Nate bashfully glanced up from his plate and sent a shy smile around the room. "Wouldn't wanna poison ya."

And again we all laughed. Breakfast turned out well.

But when we went to Zander's room to pack, the tone changed. Just seeing the suitcases set Nate off. He stood awkwardly near the doorway and said, "I gotta do a couple errands and shit. Got one last check to be cashed and—"

"Nate, it's *Sunday*. You can't cash a check today." Zander went into the hallway, came back with a big yellow duffle bag, and dropped it at Nate's feet. "Time to pack, big guy."

"But... I... uh...." A typical Nate response.

"You're coming with us, so there's no point in arguing." Zander turned back to his own suitcase. "Fill it."

For a minute or two, Nate stared at the duffle bag, looking fearful, like it might bite him. "I don't have no money."

"I have money," I offered brightly. "Most of the money I made from my summer job at Abercrombie & Fitch is still in my account."

"I got cash from my movie theater job too, dude. No worries, okay?"

Nate shifted his weight from foot to foot, clearly uncomfortable with accepting help from us.

"You'll be our 'kept man.'" I grinned at him.

"Shit," was all he said. "Can't come with ya."

That was all it took for Zander and me to drop our clothing, grab Nate, yank him over to the bed, and push him down.

"You look at me, buddy." Zander clearly meant business, so Nate looked at him. "We fucking love you, dude. We plan on having you with us for the long haul. There's gonna be times I'm gonna need your backing—your money and your strength. And I wanna know it'll be there for me when I need it. Man, it's just your turn to need right now."

I knew the moment had come for me to speak up. "And I've already been in that emotional place where I needed you guys to support me. And the support was given. The tables are turning, Nate, and we'll support you. But over a lifetime, the tables will turn over and over. We'll all be called on to support each other."

"We're a throuple." Zander looked at me and winked because he was using my term for our threesome. "Let's start acting like one. Now pack, Nate." And just like that Zander turned back to his suitcase, and I did the same.

Nate didn't argue. He filled the duffle with his clean clothes.

22
NATE'S DIARY

November 30

EVERYTHING'S SO fucked up, but in a real good way. See, these two dudes—my boyfriends, my partners, my lovers, my throuple, or whatever the fuck ya wanna call 'em—are, like, *takin' care of me*. Takin' damn good care of me too.

Better care than I ever took of myself.

Right now them two's in class, but I got strict instructions on exactly where to have my ass sittin' at lunchtime, ready and waitin'. They expect me there so we can all chow down together—it seems to mean somethin' to them—which doesn't suck. Both Casey and Zander got "food points" on these credit-card thingies that they use to get meals, and they just buy me whatever the fuck I wanna eat with them. It's cool.

And who'd of ever guessed that I'd be fuckin' *livin'* with them two in this tiny dorm room? We got the beds pushed together, and my shit is in the bottom drawers of each of those guys' dressers. I said I'd live outta the duffle bag, but they said I ain't no guest, so no fuckin' way. So yeah, I live here now. But it's just temporary.

Miz Minton is taking care of all the details with signin' me up for cookin' school. All I had to do was get Benjamin Franklin High School to send over my transcripts and fill out the official Boston Culinary Institute forms that came to me in e-mails. Miz Minton is as awesome as her son. She treats me good as gold. Plus, I'm so psyched about cookin' school. Can't believe I'm not gonna have to be no gas pumper no more.

Same with Mr. Minton. He rocks, totally. The guy's already found four apartments for us three to look at this weekend, ones that we could move into January 1.

The only thing I got left to worry over is Cindy and the fact that she still won't talk to me. I just talked to Aunt Terri yesterday, and she told me Cindy ain't softened up none in regard to me. But Casey says us three are gonna talk shit out about what went down with Cindy, cuz he tells me now I'm "emotionally ready to go there," and they're gonna help me figure this all out. They tell me that a few things were screwed up with the way Cindy had been treating *me* before all this shit went down, cuz she was always settin' me up to get beat on by Uncle Rich. So at some point we're gonna go to Cindy and try talkin' to her all together as "one voice." Plus they wanna talk to me about why I never drew the line and called the police and the reasons why they didn't either. That's all cool.

And guess what? This dumbass believes it can maybe work out. Got faith in my guys.

I was fucked up, in a real bad way, when they found me last week. It sure does seem longer than that. But I'd lost all my will to go on. Guess I was pretty sure I had nothin' to go on for. Cindy was gone, my throuple was history, couldn't support myself no more. I had no reasons.

But I was real wrong. Cuz I had lots of reasons, just didn't know where to look for 'em. I could've lost everything back then, and look what I'd be missin'. The greatest love in my life, ever.

Learned that nobody should give up when it looks dark and foggy and ugly in his life. Cuz the sun can still come out and shine again, like it did for me. Guess I'm a poet now, huh?

Been lower than low, but I'm feelin' so much better. Hopeful, even.

This Sunday night us three are goin' to the One Voice meetin' together. Those two cool girls, Claire and Anna, are gonna be there too. Zander asked me if I'd share my message about how people shouldn't give up hope, even when everything looks like it's gone to hell in a friggin' handbasket. And I'm gonna do it. Cuz I know I ain't the only one to feel that low. It might make somebody feel less shitty to know I been there too. *And* it's a real good message. Plus Zander really wants me to do this.

Kinda got a life again, don't I? Maybe I even got a message to put out there.

ZANDER ZANE'S One Voice Blog Spot—by invite only

Your host, Zander Z

December 4

One Voice Site First Official Blog Post

Hi, all. I would like to welcome you to the first official post of the Boston City College One Voice Club Blog Spot.

*Please note: There will be some back blog posts from the very beginning of the school year, but I need to sort through them. So watch the blog for "Looking Back—One Voice's First Three Months at BCC."

*Hint: There will even be a few pictures (watch out, Britta!!)

*And now you all have my phone number and my e-mail address, so there's no excuse for being a *no-show* at any meeting or event, is there? (Cue the evil laughter) Mwah ha ha!!

*Tonight, Sunday, December 4, at the weekly One Voice meeting at Boston City College, One Voice member and my partner, Nate DeMarco, spoke bravely about holding on to hope in your darkest days. He told an extremely private story of how he thought he'd lost everything—only to find that he had more than he'd ever dreamed. And make no mistake—Nate's problems have not yet been fully resolved, but he has found the motivation he needs to go on.

I'm incredibly proud of Nate for offering this intensely personal testimony to our twenty-seven One Voice members. My hope is that we all internalize it and then share it with those who need to hear it. As we well know, many of our LGBTQ brothers and sisters could use an inspirational story about not giving up at difficult points in their lives.

*To review Nate's statement in its entirety, please check the attached document, where it has been transcribed into written form. (Thank you, Casey)

*One Voice will be holding our first "Annual Holiday Gathering for Everyone" at DeSalle Hall on Friday, December 16, at 8:00 p.m. We will play get-to-know-each other games, do mad libs, eat fruitcake, and maybe even sing songs. Yes. Good, old-fashioned holiday fun. The entrance fee is a wrapped toy with an index card taped to the outside that tells us what is inside.

*We need to make posters to advertise this event, as our goal is to involve as many students and friends as possible. Anyone willing to create posters please message Casey Minton on Facebook.

*Those interested in setting up for the event, please e-mail NateDeM@catchme.com.

*If you want to help with the menu, message Anna on Facebook.

*Games crew, message contact person, Claire on FB, too.

(All of our contact info is listed on the home page of the blog.)

*And if you have any questions, comments, or suggestions, you can call me, Zander Zane, at (603) 555-1235, message me on FB, or e-mail me at zanderZ@catchme.com. Or just grab me in the hall or snag me on the quad. Just reach out to me, and I'm there.

We have come so far since the end of August, and I don't know about you, but I'm gonna party it up big time.

*Important note: This is a dry party. Beverages will include root beer and hot apple cider—and not the spiked kind. We will get high on life without the help of controlled substances.

Zander Zane

23
Nate's Diary

December 6

NOT SURE where I got the balls from, but I spoke up at the One Voice meetin' the other night. I was scared shitless to stand in front of that group of college kids and say something. But I was scared worse not to.

Here's why. I wasn't back on my game yet from what went down over the past few weeks. I hadn't found a zone where I could relax, seein' as I was still all uptight over what went down with Cindy, as well as with Zander and Casey. I lost her, and I almost fuckin' lost them, and that wigged me out to the max.

But somethin' else wigged me out even more than those things. And that was the fact that last week, right before Casey and Zander found me, I really didn't give a shit if I saw another mornin'. I admitted that sorry fact to Zander and Casey over Thanksgiving weekend.

So, yeah, standin' up in front of a crowd to talk about anything was friggin' terrifyin' for me, cuz it goes against my nature, but standin' up to talk about my feelin's was near impossible. I did it, though, cuz I was so thankful. Thankful those two found me and saved me from freezin' to death or dehydratin' or starvin' in my truck. Then all would have been lost. My life would have been lost. And even though things could've got better someday in the future, I would've been gone and I never would've known that. And there ain't no comin' back from dead.

I'm thankful that I got a second chance. And if I could give one person, somewhere out there, a second chance by just tellin' my true and ugly story, then fuck, I was gonna do it. And I was gonna do it ASAP.

Who knew what a desperate person might go and do tomorrow? So I got up there in front of those twenty-six other members, and I spilled my guts.

I told kinda like a circle of a story, startin' when I was all in love and cozy visitin' with my two guys here at school, and then movin' on, in real general terms. All I said was my little sister got beat up and I blamed it on myself. Then how I found myself alone—no little sister, no job, no home, no food, no water, no boyfriends, no love. And then I told about how them two saved me, even though I didn't ask to be saved. In fact I'd told them to get the hell outta my life. And how now I'm so damn glad they saved me.

I got lots to live for, I told them. *I got cookin' school and Casey's family, and I got the hearts of these two guys right here. And I could've lost it all because I gave up hope.*

I did my part by tellin' what I been through. I feel good about it too.

I'd say each member of One Voice hugged me twice—and tight too. They really valued my story. A couple of them came up to me and said they'd been that low themselves a time or two, and some others told me they had the perfect person to tell my story to, who really needed to hear it. I spread a message about keepin' hope alive.

Shit. I feel damn good about what I done.

Zander and Casey think I'm gonna be ready soon, as Casey says, "emotionally speaking," to talk to Aunt Terri about seein' Cindy. But us three, we're gonna talk to Aunt Terri together. Zander says we'll be one voice or no voice at all, so I ain't got nothin' to fear.

zanderZ@catchme.com

Hey, bro.

I know you were probably expecting a new One Voice blog entry, since I posted one last Sunday, but I feel like I have One

Voice on a good solid path, and I need to do everything I can to get Nate on a solid path too.

Nate really, like in a majorly bad way, wants to get back in contact with his little sister. Casey and I are bound and determined to at least try to make all of Nate's smallest wishes become reality. But that girl is not budging from her Nate-is-no-longer-my-brother stance. She actually doesn't even refer to him as "Nate." Nate's Aunt Terri told us she refers to him as "the *N* word." Yup, it's that bad between those two.

Personally, if I were Nate, I'd give Cindy a little bit of time. She clearly had a ton of anger in her even before this whole thing happened, probably because her mother got hauled off to jail and left her in a crappy excuse for a home, and she felt abandoned. Whatever the case may be, Cindy caused trouble with their uncle and stood by to watch Nate take the fall. I think Nate can see that now, but he can't bring himself to get pissed at her.

But Nate giving Cindy time—well, that's not gonna happen. The dude's losing his marbles over his little sister. He's chomping at the bit to see her, to talk to her, and to be forgiven by her. And he has so damn much faith in me and Casey, that we can wave our magic wands and fix this situation for him. So last night we piled onto the pushed-together beds, put Aunt Terri and Cindy on speakerphone, and tried to talk to Cindy. The girl's kinda immature, it seems to me. But then I don't have much experience with fourteen-year-old girls yet. I'll get more experience as I do my practicums for my degree, but right now I'm at a loss. Maybe she *is* acting perfectly normal for fourteen and female.

Cindy won't talk directly to Nate. She will talk only to her aunt and a little bit to Casey and me, but never to the so-called "*N* word."

Nate kind of shrivels up and dies a bit with every conversation. Last night's discussion went something like this:

"So... uh... Cindy... uh, just wanted to see how your new school's treatin' ya." I could tell it took every bit of courage Nate could summon to ask her that.

Long tension-filled silence, seeming extralong over the phone.

"Um... Cindy? Ya still there?"

"Aunt Terri, would you do me a small favor?" Cindy's voice was still quite raspy, a lingering result of the brush with death by strangulation she'd experienced, courtesy of Uncle Rich, but she still managed to sound haughty. "Tell the person who just asked me a question that school is school and at least I'm alive to get educated. No thanks to him."

Aunt Terri didn't relay the message. She knew we all heard it.

"Cindy," I interjected. "Nate did the best job he could to keep you safe, for years and—"

"Well, Zander, it looks like it was an epic fail for 'the *N* word,'" seeing as I turned blue in my own kitchen and then peed myself before I fell down, unconscious."

On the bed beside me, Casey reached for Nate's hand, which was trembling. I wouldn't have put it past Nate to turn blue and pee *himself,* right there and then. He was devastated by Cindy's response.

I tried again. "Hey, Cindy, listen up. Nate did everything he could to put himself between you and Rich and—"

"Everything but the one *right* thing that could have saved me from what happened, which was calling the police on our asshole uncle, on one of the last ten times he beat bleep out of 'the *N* word's' ass and threatened mine."

What she said was true, and we'd tried to tell him that a thousand times, but he thought he was doing what was right for Cindy.

"People make mistakes, Cindy. Nate is only just a human being. And you didn't exactly make it easy on him, back when you lived with your uncle." Casey's voice, as always, sounded ultrasweet, even as he defended Nate. "Remember, Cindy, Nate isn't the one who abandoned you. Your mother is the one who was put in prison."

Cindy had no snarky response to that.

Casey continued, "Terri, we thought maybe we could all get together and swap Christmas gifts on one of the coming weekends.

All we need is a time and a date, and Nate would like a list of what you all want for gifts."

Aunt Terri stammered her answer. "Well, y-you can be sure I-I'll discuss that idea with Cindy. It sounds fine to me."

"Aunt Terri," Cindy said so sweetly that it was hard to believe the voice came from out of the same girl's mouth. "Can you tell Casey to tell 'the *N* word' that it'll be a cold day in hell when that happens?"

Seeing that this conversation was essentially going in circles—and torturous circles for Nate—I decided it was time to call it a night. "Terri, we'll call back on Wednesday night… to ah… set a date, time, and place."

I couldn't miss the way Nate flopped onto the bed, defeated. He curled in on himself, and seeing that, Casey allowed a freaked-out gasp.

But before I could even blink, Casey was hovering over Nate. "Sweetheart, we'll figure this out. Don't worry."

The fetal ball on the bed didn't reply.

So I took a shot. "Nate, her issues and your issues are separate. Completely separate." I massaged the back of his neck with my thumb and my forefinger, and I did it really hard. I felt his muscles fighting back against me. "You're a convenient scapegoat right now. It's easy to blame you for all of her past pain. She knows you did your best to do what was right for her. Nate, she knows."

I expected Nate to remain tightly wrapped up inside himself and his troubles and refuse to let us in. But Nate shocked me. He unfolded from his tight ball and looked at me.

"Okay." He exhaled deeply before fully relaxing his body. "Okay, I believe what you guys are saying. Gonna have belief that this will work out good, in time."

I almost couldn't believe my ears.

"Could you guys lie down beside me, though? Cuz I could sure use some holdin'."

Instead of making us chase him, Nate had just turned to us. His instinct had told him to curl into a tight ball and hide, but his better judgment told him to enlist our help. We'd clearly made progress in helping Nate to understand that he could lean on us, and for that I was happy.

So Dan, got any suggestions on how to reach Cindy? Nate is doing okay, but I think his Christmas would be happier if Cindy were a part of it.

Your bro

Z

CASEY'S REAL LIFE

TODAY WE went to the mall. I was pretty excited. I love shopping in general, but there's something extra special about visiting a shopping center during the holiday season when it is so richly decorated. I relished that bit of frenzy in the air, but Nate and Zander weren't so enthralled with mall madness at Christmastime. That didn't stop me from cracking the figurative "shopping whip" behind those two.

"Even though shopping ranks among my least favorite things to do, Casey, I've got to admit you had an awesome idea."

A shopping compliment from Zander? I'll take it.

"Hope like hell it works," Nate said with far less emotion than I knew he felt.

"It will. If there is one thing I know, it's teenage girls." I shuddered as I said that, and the significance of my words was not lost on Nate and Zander. They'd been right there when a certain teenage girl had taken me down in a particularly violent manner. I had largely moved beyond that, but I didn't believe one could ever leave bullying and assault *completely* in one's past. "Now, where are we meeting Anna and Claire? Because they actually *are* teenage girls, if not older ones, and they know more than even I do in terms of what gifts would mean the most from Cindy's older brother."

"We're meeting them in front of that pretzel place in the food court." Zander nudged Nate in the ribs. "I'm still working on getting our big guy back to size."

Nate had filled out some since we'd gotten back together at Thanksgiving, but he still had a way to go before we could call him burly again. "Zander, get him a large order of those cinnamon-covered ones. He can't resist them."

Nate allowed a crooked smile and a blush. No matter how much he protested, Zander and I knew he loved being pampered. We found the pretzel place in no time, and Zander headed up to the counter.

"So, let's think back to what you and Zander got me when I was hurting so badly after Liz assaulted me." It was still difficult to say the words. I could tell it was also hard for Nate to hear them, as he grimaced.

"Well, one thing that's stuck in my mind is we stuffed everything inside of that big sleigh. But first we took it and painted it like a rainbow so it'd be real pretty and cheerful," Nate reminded me.

I smiled because I remembered like it was yesterday. "It was amazing. So we have to find the perfect thing to put Cindy's presents in. Or, you know, I still have the rainbow sleigh in my bedroom at home. Maybe I could have Mom bring it when she visits later this week."

"Shit. We could use that sleigh, and it would rock." By the wide grin he wore, I could tell Nate liked that idea. "Cindy loves rainbows. She was always drawing them in her school notebooks."

"That will be perfect. And you guys got me a beautiful blanket, and a T-shirt, and music, and—"

"A stuffed animal. Shit. Cindy goes nuts for real cute stuffed animals."

"What else does she like?"

His brow furrowed up in deep thought. "She likes tight jeans. And she likes chocolate."

"Well, then, I have a few ideas."

Zander came back and handed Nate a large cup of cinnamon pretzel nuggets, all warm from the heat lamp. "Eat these, dude. And I stole one, just saying."

Nate held a nugget out to me. "You want one, Casey?"

I opened my mouth wide and let him feed it to me, thinking I could get used to that treatment.

Once Anna and Claire made their appearance, shopping began in earnest. The two girls headed to the American Eagle store to buy the least personal of gifts, the gift card, so Cindy could pick out her own jeans. Zander, Nate, and I headed to the jewelry store.

As we stood there, gazing at the necklaces in the glass case, Nate muttered, "We can't get Cindy one of these things. They gotta be way too expensive. Look. They got all the price tags flipped over so we can't see 'em and that spells big bucks. They don't want us to fall over from the shock of seein' the high prices on the stickers."

Zander placed his hand on Nate's shoulder. "Don't sweat it, man. We got your back. And remember, there's gonna come a time I need you to have my back."

We all looked at the silver heart-shaped locket that Nate seemed to like best.

"I'm gonna put a picture of me when I was just a kid and Cindy when she was little on the two sides of the locket, so she'll look at 'em and remember what we been through together."

As we walked down the length of the mall, heading toward the toy store, I could tell that Nate was genuinely excited when I said, "So now it's time for you to pick out the cutest stuffed animal of all stuffed animals."

Nate headed straight for the plush animals. I mean, he pretty much ran. By the time Zander and I caught up to him, he had a teddy bear in one hand and a little dog in the other, and he was looking back and forth, from one to the other, with the most serious expression on his face.

"What are you doing there, dude?" Zander stepped up beside him. "And let me tell you a secret, you can ask those stuffed animals all the questions you want—they aren't gonna answer you."

Nate blushed furiously. "I'm just studyin' them to figure out which one has the cutest face and the most sorry expression. See." He held out the dog so we could see its face. "This guy is fuckin' adorable, right?" We nodded. Then he held out the bear. "But this guy looks like he's super sorry."

"Why don't you get her both?" I figured that would solve the problem.

Nate looked to Zander for approval, and Zander was ready with it. "That'll surely let her know how much you care, Nate."

Breathing a huge sigh of relief, Nate practically sprinted to the cash register, Nate and I close on his heels.

We met up with the girls at the only sit-down restaurant in the food court. Shopping bags were stuffed between us on the booths, and we sat like we used to before we broke up, with me in the middle and both of my guys' arms around me.

"We picked out this shirt for her." Claire held up an adorable tie-front pink cotton blouse. "But if you don't like it, we can return it."

"And these pj's, which match with these slippers." All fuzzy and aqua. Cindy's favorite color.

"Sweet!" Nate was actually enthusiastic—at a shopping mall. There's a first time for everything.

"And girls, check out this blanket we picked out for Cindy at JCPenney." Zander pulled out a soft zebra-striped throw blanket. "It's heated."

Nate was breathless. He pulled his arm from my back and reached out to grab the blanket from Zander's hand. Then he held it to his chest. He even closed his eyes.

"Nate, my man." Zander must have experienced the very same feeling of trepidation that I did. "You know, giving Cindy these gifts might not fix everything overnight. Right?"

"Look at it as a first step." Claire obviously knew what Zander was getting at.

And then I took my turn at warning him. "Remember Christmas of my junior year, after the assault, you guys gave me gifts, and I truly loved them. I cherished them because they gave me hope." I fastened my gaze to his. "But I didn't make any attempt to get in touch with you guys. I wasn't ready, at that point."

In response, he nodded solemnly. "Gotcha, Casey." He handed the throw blanket back to Zander just as the waitress approached our table. "I guess we oughtta order."

24
Nate's Diary

December 16

AFTER CLASSES on Tuesday, us three drove to Aunt Terri's house in Somerton to deliver the sleigh full of presents for my little sister. Yesterday, Miz Minton came to visit us, and like the saint she is, she brought the big sleigh with her. She stuck it in the backseat of her car. And after she gave it to us, she took us out for a breakfast-sorta dinner. We all had these stuffed omelets and homemade toast. There are actually kids with folks who'll come and visit just to say hi and do you a favor and for no other reason. Yeah, wonders never cease.

On purpose, we set it up so we'd deliver the big present when Cindy wasn't home. Casey told me it'd put less pressure on her that way, and I agreed, even though it sucked. We also brought Aunt Terri a gourmet coffee cake from a way cool bakery near BCC, and we got my cousin, Jana, the same kinda chocolates that we got for Cindy from this upscale candy shop in the city. I was fuckin' hopeful as hell when I dropped off them gifts, thinkin' Cindy'd take one look at her big present-filled sleigh and rush to her cell phone to call me, but that didn't happen.

It's been three days now, and I ain't heard word one from the girl. At least Aunt Terri called to say the coffee cake was the best she ever tasted. And Jana liked the candy. She got on the phone for a couple seconds to tell me that.

But nope, no word from Cindy. Casey said that sometimes these things take time.

Tonight is the One Voice holiday party, and Zander's all nervous to be holdin' such a fancy event. But me and Casey got his back, cuz that's what partners do for each other.

So I'm waitin' on Cindy's phone call. And sure, it sucks to wait. But my life is goin' on, and tomorrow we're even gonna go look at some apartments that Mr. Minton found for us three to live in, all together. And then we're gonna get a couple pieces of furniture—like a big bed and a kitchen set—to go in our new place. The brand-new furniture is gonna be the Mintons' big Christmas gift to us three.

When I think of Mr. and Miz Minton—this is gonna sound pretty fucked up—but I kinda automatically think "Mom" and "Dad." Even more fucked up than me thinkin' it, is that I think the Mintons would kinda like to know that. They'd be glad.

Maybe soon I'll tell 'em.

So, as far as Cindy goes, I just keep on waitin' and givin' her the time she needs to be ready.

Zander and Casey say it'll be okay. I believe them two.

ONE VOICE Blog Spot—by invite only

Your host, Zander Z

December 17

Stellar holiday get-together, fellow One Voicers. We had thirty-two cool, awesome, open-minded people in attendance on Friday night. Way to go, us!

*The big guy stationed at the door, Nate DeMarco, collected *forty*—yes, you heard me right, *forty*—wrapped kids' holiday presents as entry fees. Apparently some of you went above and beyond the call of duty by bringing more than one gift. (*Thank you, kindly.*) One Voice is a can-collecting, gift-giving force to be reckoned with in the Boston area. And I'm putting an article with pictures—consider this fair warning—into the BCC Gazette about the One Voice Holiday Party and the huge donation we made to the Boston Chapter of the Presents for Young People Campaign.

*On a personal note, as the holidays approach, I would like to take the time to thank some important people in my life.

*First and foremost—my partners, Casey and Nate, I wake up smiling every day because of you guys. Love is love, and we got a ton of it between the three of us.

*Dan, my bro, you are always there with big ears—nuff said.

*Abby, you make my bro happy, and that's so cool.

*Claire and Anna, sisters, friends, confidantes, organizers. Never before had friends like you.

*Mr. and Mrs. Minton, you guys are the parents Nate and I never had. Love the apartment we picked out together today. Loved that Lola and Sarah gave it the stamp of approval, even though I think that was only because they fell in love with the black cat on the window seat.

*My fellow One Voice members, you have helped me to realize my dream of establishing an enduring alliance that will ensure that all people, regardless of their sexual identity, will feel safe and welcome on the Boston City College campus.

Superstoked to see where we'll go as a group next year with our one strong voice.

Zander Zane, president of One Voice BCC

25
NATE'S DIARY

December 20

WELL, WE kinda said good-bye to "our" college dorm room in a real proper way last night. Best thing is, Zander says we're gonna say hello to our new apartment down the street in just the same way. ☺

So anyhow, we said our good-byes on that pushed-together bed. All around us everything was packed up. My yellow duffle bag was stuffed full of my clothes, and Casey and Zander had all of their shit stuck into, like, six big boxes that were shoved against the wall. Only thing that hadn't got packed yet was the set of red sheets that were underneath our bare asses on the bed.

We started out kinda in a circle made outta our bodies, layin' on our sides and lookin' at each other. Casey was busy playin' with my toes, Zander was runnin' his hand through my hair at the other end, and I was doin' the same kinda shit to them two.

Casey looked at me and said, real serious, "We're so glad to have you back, sweetheart. And I think I speak for both of us when I say, we... we want you to make love to us tonight." That was real direct, but I got why he said it.

Don't know just why, but lately most of our foolin' around had involved more our hands and our mouths and less full-out makin' love. It was like we *wanted* to go all the way, but before we could get there, we got so caught up in holdin' each other and rubbin' on each other that we spent ourselves too soon. But Casey let me know that he wanted that night to be different. Zander was noddin' at me too, so I got the feelin' he was right on board with Casey.

I suddenly got this rush of want, and it wasn't the kinda want I expected it'd be, seein' as we were stark naked on the bed. It wasn't just a physical wantin' to get busy with them. I wanted to make these two feel as loved and as worshipped as they made me feel. I wanted to be in charge of their sexual feelin's, top to bottom. And I wanted it to be *my show*—so they would know when they were givin' up the best come of their lives, that their big Nate gave it to 'em.

"Lay flat on your backs." Didn't trust my voice too much, but the words ended up comin' out just fine. Almost like a command. And I could tell by the way they looked at each other with eyes all wide that they liked it. "Hold hands and put the other one under your ass."

Them two did just as I asked, and they did it real fast. No joke, the three of us was all ready to go. Each of us was so rock hard we were ready to perform, but it was all up to me. I especially liked watchin' Zander scramble to obey me. Turned me on in a big way.

Soon as they were lyin' there holdin' hands, I did my thing. My lips were itchin' to kiss 'em, but I wasn't gonna start with their lips like they expected. Nope, I went right downstairs on 'em. Startin' with Zander. He friggin' whimpered when I took his dick in my mouth. Casey whimpered too, and my mouth wasn't nowhere near his junk. That was too fuckin' cute.

Took turns on my guys, didn't touch 'em or nothin' when my mouth was on the other. I let 'em wait their turn. Built up the wantin' in 'em.

Didn't take too long before they were startin' to hump up into my mouth, and I knew I had to move on to other activities unless I wanted them shootin' before I got inside.

Figured I'd do Casey first, seein' as he was closer to goin' off. "Get on your bellies now." Grabbed the lube, got 'em both ready at once. That wasn't easy, as there was only one of me and two of them, but I got the job done just fine. And then I got on Casey. "Zander, get on your side. I want you smashed right up against us when I'm doin' Casey. I wanna feel your dick pushin' on my leg. And I want you two kissin' each other and not stoppin' 'cept for to breathe and... want your hand on his dick, but not makin him shoot 'til I give ya the say-so. Ya got me?"

Zander pushed his dick against my leg and wedged his hand under Casey's hips, makin' Casey gasp. I took that as a "Yes, sir."

And then us three went to town. When I gave the word and Casey shot, I had to friggin' hold myself back from doin' the same right inside him, cuz I hadn't given Zander his attention yet. But Casey friggin' moaned, and then me and Zander moaned right along with him, cuz we knew Casey felt so good.

"I did that to you cuz I love you, Casey. Now it's Zander's turn. Casey, help us out here."

My guys switched places real quick while I cleaned myself off and got ready to take Zander. Casey had paid attention, and he knew just what to do. When Zander got onto his belly and I climbed on, Casey pressed his whole body against us, started mumbling words of love, and grabbed Zander's junk with his hand. It was friggin' hard not to just explode in Zander right when I got inside, but I managed to keep control. Me and Casey brought him to the best come of his life.

"I love you, Zander. Always gonna. It's us three."

Casey got on his knees and took my face in his soft hands, and he started kissin' me so tender. And that's when I went off into Zander.

Never felt like that. Never felt so close to Casey and Zander.

I fuckin' broke down and cried. Yup, big old Nate DeMarco crumpled onto the bed, pulled my lovers down on top of me, and bawled.

Them two kissed me—all three of our lips pushed together at once—until I stopped with the tears.

CASEY'S REAL LIFE

WE HAD the back of Nate's truck completely packed with our stuff. If Santa drove a truck, it would look like this. We were heading back to my house. The three of us were going to stay together in my room for the college holiday break, and then we'd move into our new apartment. We weren't ready to be apart for even a few days, and especially not for Christmas. We belonged together, and we knew it.

So overall, there was a happy feeling in the truck. Zander was thrilled with the first semester's progress with One Voice, and I was overjoyed that I was on a path to straight As. Nate was excited that my mother had set him up to start culinary school in late January.

More than any of those things, though, we were thrilled that we were together to begin with, and that we had signed a lease for a cute one-bedroom apartment between the two campuses. The three of us would live as one unit, and all of us agreed that there was nothing better.

"We used one voice, Nate. You know, we sent our message to Cindy *together* in all of those phone calls. Even the Christmas gift to Cindy had all of our names on it." Zander spoke to the subject that was on all our minds, the one thing preventing us from experiencing complete, unfettered holiday joy. "The three of us together, we did our best. Now it's up to her."

It had been over a week since we'd delivered the sleigh filled with gifts to Cindy. There had been no word from her. But Nate seemed to like the fact that all three of us were equally invested in rekindling his relationship with Cindy. He probably felt less alone.

"I know I needed a little bit of time after I received your gifts during junior year in high school. Serious emotional pain, Nate, builds up over time. Her pain and anger have built up over years of an unstable home life, with your mom going to jail and with your uncle's violence. You tried to make it stable for her. But you were a kid too, for most of those years. And I really think she has misplaced her anger at those other factors and directed it at you and...." I was rambling, which was what I did best. And since I was between Zander and Nate, I put a hand on each of their knees. "Cindy's in a stable place now. And when she's ready, she'll have *three* big brothers to spoil her."

That got Nate to smile. "Thanks, you guys." He took one of those deep breaths that usually precedes a loud sigh. But instead of sighing, he said, "Guess I'm bummed cuz this'll be my first Christmas not seein' her, that's all." He placed his big hand on mine and squeezed. "But I got you guys, so I'm all good. And that's the truth." Nate glanced away from the highway for a split second, just long enough to meet our eyes.

After a brief silence, Zander asked, "Wanna stop for fries from Mickey D's?"

Zander had a thing for junk food lately, but I think really he wanted to just move to a different topic. There was no point dwelling on Cindy. The ball—Zander had reminded us that morning—was in her court.

"Sure, I can stop at the Mickey D's right offa the highway."

As soon as Nate stopped speaking, his cell phone beeped. He'd received a text message, which was odd, because Zander and I were about the only two who ever texted Nate.

"My phone's in my pocket." Nate dug inside the right front pocket of his jeans and pulled out his phone. "Will ya read it and tell me what it says, Casey?"

I took it from his hand and exchanged a quick glance and a mutual shrug with Zander. "I'd be glad to." But as soon as I saw the message on the screen, my eyes filled up, my throat got tight, and I felt like I might cry. I handed the phone to Zander, knowing I was too choked up to speak.

Zander read the message to himself, and then he reached his arm around me so his hand rested on Nate's shoulder. "It's big news, Nate. You wanna pull over?"

Nate shook his head. "Nah. I'm good." He set his chin in a resolute pose. "Just read me the thing."

Zander cleared his throat. "It's from Cindy, dude." He didn't glance at Nate, but I did. His expression remained controlled. "She wrote, 'Hey, big bro, it's your annoying little sis. Just wanted to give you and your boys a shout out. *Huge thank you* for my Christmas presents.'" Zander hesitated while Nate absorbed that much. "Aunt Terri is having some kind of big to-do on Christmas Eve, and she wants you and Zander and Casey to come to her house for it. I told her I'd deliver the message. So what do you say, bro? You up for Christmas Eve with your bitchy baby sister? Let me know. And no, I don't hate your butt. So stop thinking that. Cindy."

A couple of seconds later another text came in from Cindy, and again Zander dutifully read it aloud. "Lately, I been talking a lot to Aunt Terri, and she made me see that what happened to me wasn't your fault. And that some of what happened to you before mighta been partly *my* fault. Like how I always pissed Uncle Rich off to get him going, not caring and fully knowing you'd take the heat for it. I been thinking a lot on why I acted that way. Hope we can talk about it in person."

And Nate just sat there, wearing a blank expression. We both stared at him. This was what he'd been waiting for—longing for—and he wasn't screaming "woohoo" or fist-bumping us one by one or even changing the stern set of his lips into a grin.

"Dude, Cindy wants to see you... on Christmas Eve...."

"Why aren't you going nuts, sweetheart?"

Nate then, very calmly, put his turn signal on and pulled over to the shoulder of the highway. Once he came to a stop, he dropped his head onto the steering wheel and froze in that position.

"Nate." I could feel it coming. I was about to start chattering in an effort to break the moment of intense quiet.

But before I could do that, Nate lifted his head and turned in the driver's seat so he could face us. His dark eyes were narrowed slightly, and I'd never seen them more intense.

"You guys... *my* guys...." Nate's voice broke, and he cleared his throat. "I'm super glad Cindy wants to spend Christmas Eve with me—*with us*. But it just kinda hit me. If I got you guys, I got what I need to go on."

I wasn't expecting a confession like that. What happened with Cindy had been what had nearly sent him over the edge.

"See, she's my sister, and she means a ton to me. But you guys are...." He took another one of those deep breaths, and then he forced himself to squeak out the words. "You guys are part of my heart. Can't *feel* nothin' without ya."

"Our hearts, dude, are all wrapped up together. It's true for all of us." Zander's voice shook. "I need you two as much as you guys need me."

Instinctively, Zander and Nate leaned in toward me. We fumbled for a second to get our arms positioned around each other, but we managed to accomplish a successful group hug.

"I have a feeling that this is going to be a very good Christmas," I offered, needing to lighten the mood.

"A real good year," Nate added.

"A perfect life, if we stay on course. The three of us with one voice, right?" Zander said it perfectly, and we all knew it, so we nodded.

And then Nate pulled the truck back onto the highway. I couldn't keep myself from chattering about places we were going to go over Christmas break. I had made a list. Zander just smiled, and I was almost positive that Nate mumbled, "Never going nowhere else without you guys."

Don't miss

Us Three
(Published by
Harmony Ink Press)

One Voice: Book One

By Mia Kerick

In his junior year at a public high
school, sweet, bright Casey
Minton's biggest worry isn't being gay. Keeping from being too
badly bullied by his so-called friends, a group of girls called the
Queen Bees, is more pressing. Nate DeMarco has no friends, his
tough home life having taken its toll on his reputation, but he's
determined to get through high school. Zander Zane's story is
different: he's popular, a jock. Zander knows he's gay, but fellow
students don't, and he'd like to keep it that way.

No one expects much when these three are grouped together for a
class project, yet in the process the boys discover each other's
talents and traits, and a new bond forms. But what if Nate, Zander,
and Casey fall in love—each with the other and all three together?
Not only gay but also a threesome, for them high school becomes
infinitely more complicated and maybe even dangerous. To survive
and keep their love alive, they must find their individual strengths
and courage and stand together, honest and united. If they can do
that, they might prevail against the Queen Bees and a student body
frightened into silence—and even against their own crippling fears.

http://www.harmonyinkpress.com

MIA KERICK is the mother of four exceptional children—all named after saints—and four nonpedigreed cats—all named after the next best thing to saints, Boston Red Sox players. Her husband of twenty-two years has been told by many that he has the patience of Job, but don't ask Mia about that, as it is a sensitive subject.

Mia focuses her stories on the emotional growth of troubled young men and their relationships, and she believes that physical intimacy has a place in a love story, but not until it is firmly established as a love story. As a teen, Mia filled spiral-bound notebooks with romantic tales of tortured heroes (most of whom happened to strongly resemble lead vocalists of 1980s big-hair bands) and stuffed them under her mattress for safekeeping. She is thankful to Dreamspinner Press for providing her with an alternate place to stash her stories.

Mia cheers for each and every victory made in the name of marital equality, embraces the spirit of true Christianity that focuses on loving one another, and can barely keep up with the idea factory that is her mind. Her stories are often centered around a certain theme: even heroes can be sweet. Sweet, but not completely innocent. Her only major regret: never having taken typing or computer class in school, destining her to a life consumed with two-fingered pecking and constant prayer to the Gods of Technology.

Contact Mia at miakerick@gmail.com. Come visit http://www.miakerick.com for updates on what is going on in Mia's world, rants, music, parties, and pictures, and maybe even a little bit of inspiration.

Beggars and Choosers

By Mia Kerick

After a hard life filled with experiences he'd rather not remember but can't forget, Brett Taylor decides he doesn't need anyone or anything. He gets a job at a bar in a nothing little town where he can fish and race dirt bikes and hide from the world. So naturally as he's walking across the parking lot at his new job, reminding himself how self-reliant he is, he meets someone he can't shove aside.

Brett can't help but admire Cory Butana, the kid who lives above the bar where his father is the principal bartender. Unwanted by either parent, the sweet, personable Cory grew up neglected and hungry for affection. Now he's determined to make something of his life, even if he has to work himself ragged to do it.

Cory shouldn't have to suffer like Brett did, and Brett wants to lend a hand. But when their relationship evolves into something Brett isn't ready to need, he reacts… and the consequences may destroy their fledgling future. With scars like theirs, forgiveness is never easy.

http://www.dreamspinnerpress.com

Unfinished Business

By Mia Kerick

After struggling through dishonesty, betrayal, and the kind of pasts they'd like to leave behind them, Brett Taylor and Cory Butana are back together and starting to build a new life. Brett has a good job. Cory has started college. But not everything goes the way they planned.

Still recovering from the emotional and physical repercussions of a brutal assault, Cory finds himself trapped by his own insecurity and fear, unable to believe that his heart is safe with Brett or that his body is safe without him. On the other hand, Brett has total faith in Cory's love and commitment, even though he still struggles with his own ghosts.

With girls flocking to Brett's side and a wannabe-lover lab partner feeding his doubts, Cory can't find a way to tell Brett about the unfinished business that haunts him. If Brett wants to save him, he'll have to see through Cory's deception in time.

http://www.dreamspinnerpress.com

Out of Hiding

By Mia Kerick

After graduating from high school early, twenty-year-old Philippe Bergeron spent the past several years lost among the stars while fishing off the New England coast. A shoulder injury ends his dream of living reclusively on the water, and he finds himself lost among the bright lights of New York City. His older brother, Henri, has asked Philippe to chaperone his seventeen-year-old niece, Sophie, on her tours of the city's legendary dance programs.

Sophie meets with professional dancer and choreographer, Dario Pereira, to prepare a routine for her college auditions. Dario's cool perfection and immaculate style contrast with Philippe's awkward scruffiness, but it wakes desires Philippe thought he'd left behind. When the attraction is surprisingly returned, Dario's confidence won't let Philippe remain invisible. Unsure but curious, Philippe relaxes his rule of isolation, and as the summer progresses, his relationship with Dario leads him to a surprising discovery of his submissive sexual tendencies and a greater sense of self-awareness.

Tragedy threatens to destroy the connections Philippe has made and forces him to retreat into the shadows of his past, far from the radiance of Dario's love. Ultimately, he must decide if it is time to stop hiding and set himself free.

http://www.dreamspinnerpress.com

A Package Deal

By Mia Kerick

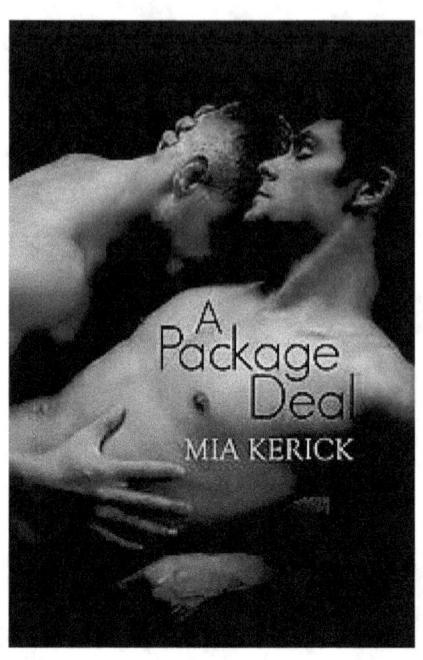

Robby Dalton is the perfect all-American boy. He played the sports his father chose for him in high school, attended the college his father selected, and has worked hard to conform to his father's macho views. But emotionally he doesn't fit anywhere, and he can't connect with a woman beyond a few uninspired dates. Robby's not in the closet, because he's never guessed he's gay. Now he owns a small commercial construction company, and one night after work he runs into Savannah Meyers. He finds her fascinating and agrees to a date, thinking maybe this woman would be different.

But Savannah has her own agenda. She is looking for a love match for her roommate, Tristan Chartrand, whom she rescued from the streets years ago. He's like a brother, and her only family, so she wants him safe and happy. Her plan seems to begin well, because when Robby meets Tristan, he's surprised to find it's Tristan he wants, not Savannah. But some people in Robby's life don't approve of Tristan's lowly station in life, and some don't approve of Robby being gay. Some people are full of hate and violence, and Robby and Tristan will need courage and strength if a loving future is to be part of the deal.

http://www.dreamspinnerpress.com

Random Acts

By Mia Kerick

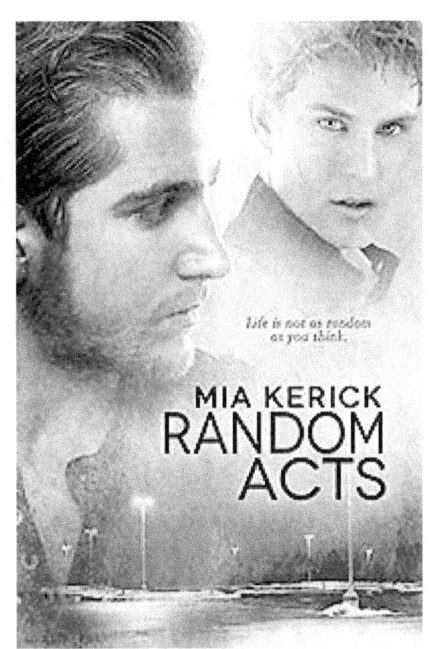

Bradley Zelder can't find his way in life. After struggling for nearly a decade, he has yet to complete his college degree. Working as a school custodian, living in blue-collar Landsbury, MA, his love life is as empty as the rest of his existence. But on his way home after another disastrous date, his truck breaks down in upscale Oceanside. When he thinks life can't get any worse, a man who is the epitome of Boston elite and everything Bradley finds attractive and intimidating helps him move his truck to the side of the road. Ashamed of his lot in life, Bradley almost lets the opportunity slip away, but he comes to his senses in time and tracks Caleb down.

From a random act of kindness, romance begins to grow, filling all the dark corners of Bradley's empty life—until a random act of violence threatens to take it all away. Bradley must step up and be the man Caleb believes him to be. Caleb rescued him from a life without hope. Can Bradley rescue him in return?

http://www.dreamspinnerpress.com

www.ingramcontent.com/pod-product-compliance
Lightning Source LLC
Chambersburg PA
CBHW070117260626
47160CB00004B/1506